A Hustler's Deceit

Aryanna

Lock Down Publications & Ca$h Presents
A Hustler's Deceit

.

Aryanna

Lock Down Publications
P.O. Box 1482
Pine Lake, Ga 30072-1482

Visit our website at **www.lockdownpublications.com**

First Edition June 2017
Printed in the United States of America
This is a work of fiction. Names, characters, places, and incidents either are products of the author's imagination or are used fictitiously. Any similarity to actual events or locales or persons, living or dead, is entirely coincidental.

Cover design and layout by: Dynasty's Cover Me
Book interior design by: Shawn Walker
Edited by: Tumika Cain

Stay Connected with Us!

Text **LOCKDOWN** to 22828 to stay up-to-date with new releases, sneak peaks, contests and more…
Or CLICK HERE to sign up.

Thank you!

Like our page on Facebook:

Lock Down Publications: Facebook

Join Lock Down Publications/The New Era Reading Group

Follow us on Instagram:

Lock Down Publications: Instagram

Email Us: We want to hear from you!

Submission Guideline.

Submit the first three chapters of your completed manuscript to ldpsubmissions@gmail.com, subject line: Your book's title. The manuscript must be in a .doc file and sent as an attachment. Document should be in Times New Roman, double spaced and in size 12 font. Also, provide your synopsis and full contact information. If sending multiple submissions, they must each be in a separate email.

Have a story but no way to send it electronically? You can still submit to LDP/Ca$h Presents. Send in the first three chapters, written or typed, of your completed manuscript to:

LDP: Submissions Dept
Po Box 1482
Pine Lake, Ga 30072

DO NOT send original manuscript. Must be a duplicate.

Provide your synopsis and a cover letter containing your full contact information.

Thanks for considering LDP and Ca$h Presents.

Acknowledgments

Father God, your blessing in times of darkness keep me hopeful for what comes next. I take nothing for granted, so I thank you first. I have to thank my amazing Belinda Diane who continues to push me to be the best at everything I do. Love isn't a big enough word for what I feel. I have to thank my Grumpy Bear and my Heart Song Bear for motivating me and loving me even on my bad days. I have to thank my fans for all their love and support, because no matter how many books I put out I remain humble because I understand that you made me. I have to thank my Grandma, Mrs. Gladys, for putting up with the headache that is me. I love you, Nana! I have to thank my beautiful Aryanna for being everything that you are. One day you'll realize how much you mean to me, and that I have always loved you. I have to thank my Lock Down Publications family for embracing me in what I love to do the most. I am ready for this ride and I know we got the juice. Lastly, I absolutely have to thank my HATERS. The shit you do is soooo helpful. I need you in my life, so don't ever change and don't get too down on yourself about my success. It's God's plan. Holla at him lol! And to anyone I didn't thank, if you feel like it's some shade…I'm sorry or not!!

Dedication

This book is dedicated to the real niggas who never see the fake ones coming. Trust no one; only give them the benefit of doubt.

Aryanna

Chapter One
Annandale, VA
April 2002

"Come on, baby, I gotta go," I said, gently trying to extract myself from her embrace.

"You've always got to go, Zay. I thought you said things would be different this time."

"Carmen, please don't start. You know I'm not in the streets like I used to be. I'm home by nine p.m. and I turn my phone off by eleven p.m., just like you asked."

"But you're still out there taking risks, babe. You should know by now that I'd rather have you than all the material things you provide." She raked her nails across my chest with just enough pressure to make my dick jump.

If it had been any other woman I was sharing a bed with I wouldn't believe that line she'd just kicked my way, but Carmen was different. We went back to the days of red light/green light and hide-n-seek. Then hide-n-seek turned into hide and go get it! Now here we are, barely nineteen, and already thirteen years of love and life together. She was my world, my beginning and ending, and spending a year away from her in county had made that crystal clear to me.

Not only had she held me down, but when necessary, she'd stood side by side in the trenches with her big brother in the streets to hold on to what was ours. Her brother, Rocko, was my right hand, and truthfully the brain behind whatever operation we got involved in. Carmen was definitely a rider, but in return for her doing that I had to do shit differently once I came home. In a show of good faith, I'd even gotten my G.E.D., and gathered information on community colleges in the surrounding northern Virginia area.

I wanted to do better and be better because that's what Carmen deserved, but as they say the road to hell is paved with good intentions. Our two bedroom high-rise apartment wasn't gonna pay for itself. Neither were the cars we drove, the clothes we rocked or the trips we loved to take on a moment's notice. Trafficking guns and selling drugs paid for all this shit and it paid well. We all had our hands in the pie and we were all addicted to the money. I knew the love we shared mattered more than anything, but I wasn't at the point where I could just abandon the life of crime. Life costs and crime pays.

"Baby, listen, the move I'm getting ready to make tonight is about putting an insurance plan in place for us. Doing that year opened my eyes to the reality that I can be taken from you, and next time it could be for a lot longer. I couldn't stand that, babe."

"Neither could I. That year...I felt so alone, Zay. I know I wasn't physically behind the wall with you, but a bitch was still doing time. I'd do it all over again, but I don't want to."

The way her shoulders slumped told me she had the weight of the world on her, and I could imagine that is the way she felt while I was gone. In her eyes I could see how tired she was, but I know in this case it was from an emotional standpoint. Because being with a man while he is doing time came with a lot of ups and downs.

"And you won't have to," I assured her, pulling her naked body against mine under the covers.

I'd thought that giving her some of this good dick would allow me to avoid the very conversation we were having, but obviously, I was wrong. Time for plan B.

"Listen, I'll only be gone an hour at the most. I promise," I said.

I pulled her beneath me kissing her neck, working my way down. Her body was flawless, and I never tired of it. She was only five foot three inches and weighed one hundred and forty pounds wet, but she fit my six foot two, hundred and thirty-pound frame perfectly. Her body was firm, yet incredibly soft, and her skin tasted like delicious peaches.

"T-that's not fair, Zay," she whispered, as my tongue danced with her left nipple and then her right, grazing both sensitive gumdrops with my teeth.

Continuing my onslaught, I navigated my way across her flat stomach, only stopping just above her love triangle where she could feel my breath teasing her skin. I gave her slow, soft kisses, knowing her body was sensitive to every drop of moisture coming from my mouth.

"Zay! Z-zavion!" she screamed when I got to her clit, making me suck on it harder as I pushed two fingers inside her throbbing pussy. I worked her at a steady rhythm, unrelenting even when her back arched in defiance of gravity.

I knew her body better than my own and when I felt the storm reach its peak I traded my fingers for my tongue, pushing her through the gates of heaven, and making her cum fiercely as she chanted the Lord's name. The taste of her in my mouth and down my throat was like giving me life, and I was tempted to serve her some more of this good loving, but I knew I had to make my move. I could tell she was exhausted.

My meeting was set for 2 a.m., which coincided with shift change, and that only gave me 20 minutes.

While she was laying there still trying to regroup I got up and put on my jeans, tee-shirt, and sneakers. I was rocking my K-mart special gear for this mission because I hated when I had to burn my good clothes.

"Will you at least tell me what the pay is?" she asked, lighting a cigarette.

"I just gotta make a drop, easy," I replied grabbing my phone and car keys.

"Is Rocko going with you?"

"Nah, I'm not traveling heavy, it's only a money thing."

"Well…"

"Don't even think about it, you not coming. Don't turn this into an argument," I warned.

Even in the dark of night I could see the fire in her eyes. Carmen had never been a pushover. Shit she was Cuban and black, which meant she came with two types of attitude. Even so, she still held her tongue. I'd probably pay for that later, but if I did this right I was at least guaranteeing that there would be a later.

There's no retirement plans for street niggas. Every minute of every day was a two-way gamble, between the grave and the penitentiary. Both liked to grab ahold of young black men, and neither had a return policy. Society saw prison as a way of paying a debt and a chance at the illusion called redemption, but society didn't see how broken a lot of mufuckas came home. I didn't want to end up like so many of my niggas who would never be more than their state number. I wasn't just in the game to survive. I was in it to win.

"I love you," I told her, kissing her gently on the forehead before making my way out of the apartment, and down to my car.

As soon as I slid behind the wheel of my '79 Eldorado my phone started vibrating in my pocket.

"Yo?" I answered.

"Where are you?"

"I'm on my way."

"Good, I'm just leaving now so we should get there at the same time. No shorts this time, Zay, I mean it."

I didn't respond, I simply flipped my phone closed, started my car, and eased out of the parking lot. I hated dealing with mufuckas in a position of authority, because they always felt like they were superior to common criminals, and the more crooked they were the more bullshit they came with. It was the way of the world though. You had to pay to play or you weren't just on borrowed time, you were a moving target.

The streets of the Dale were almost deserted at this time of the morning, but when factoring in the light rain falling it made sense. And it was to my advantage. A Cadillac the size of most SUVs sitting on twenty-four inch tires wasn't exactly inconspicuous, especially not given the area I was getting ready to cruise into. Ordinarily, me and this crooked cop would meet on my turf, or at least somewhere neutral, but in this situation, it benefitted me that he seemed to be following his normal routine of going home after work.

I made the trip to the outskirts of suburban Annandale in fifteen minutes, which gave me a few minutes to go over my plan one more time.

Pulling on my hoodie and my gloves, I grabbed the Glock .27 from under my seat, checking it to make sure it was loaded. I wouldn't have time to get to it if I tucked it in my jeans, and having it in my hoodie pocket would make it too obvious. The only thing I could think to do was to keep it in my hand and pull my sleeve over everything, hoping to sell the illusion of being cold and wet.

I had just enough time to get it done before his lights blinded me as he pulled his car nose to nose with mine.

Game time, I said to myself, grabbing the money-filled envelope and stuffing it in my hoodie pocket before stepping from my ride. With my hood down I rushed to the passenger side of his car and hopped in.

"Good to see you," he said.

"Yeah, I bet," I replied sarcastically, tossing the envelope in his lap.

"You won't mind waiting while I count it, right?"

"And if I do?"

"I don't really give a fuck. You're gonna sit there until I say it's okay to do otherwise," he replied smiling.

Inwardly, I was smiling too, despite the grit on my face. Sometimes I had to let people think shit was their idea.

"What's with this multiple denomination shit, I told you to have it all in hundreds," he complained, even though he started counting the twenty thousand dollars immediately.

"My bad, I didn't have time to go to the bank," I replied, dropping my right arm out of sight as casually as I could.

He was absorbed in his counting and not paying me any attention, which almost made it too easy to stick my arm back through my sleeve, and bring my plan one step closer to completion. It took a full 5 minutes to count the money, but it was worth the wait.

"$20,000. I appreciate your contribution," he said, putting the money back in the envelope.

"You know what, on second thought I'ma need that back," I said, bringing the gun to his temple.

"What the fuck do you think you're doing? You're not gonna shoot a cop."

"And why is that?"

"Because you're not stupid! You murder me and the world will collapse on you."

"You know, this is probably the first time we agree on something, because cop killing is a very serious thing. One day your death is gonna save my life though, so thank you," I said pulling the trigger.

Chapter Two
Powhatan Correctional Center
July 2007

"You niggas is set!" I bragged, slamming down the thirteenth spade on top of the three cards already on the table.

The truth in this declaration sent the partners to arguing again about whose fault it was that they lost another game of spades to me and my young nigga Fred. I was nice with most games involving fifty-two cards, but Fred was a monster! Only twenty years old, from Charlottesville, VA, but he handled a deck of cards like he'd lived his whole life in Vegas. He was a quiet, pretty boy type with a slim build, but behind the quick smile was the mind of a killer, and I respected him for it.

The two dudes we were playing against were from New York, which was normally enough to make us dislike them, but amazingly we were all cool. Boo Gotti was a small Puerto Rican kid with a lion's heart and the mouth to match. His partner was a tall Haitian nigga named Double Oh, who was quiet, but just as fierce. They were cut from a different cloth and a different world than me and Fred, because they were Bloods. It wasn't my place to judge, but gang bangin' made no sense to me. Then again, I didn't really try to understand it. Their money was as good as the next mufuckas, and right now they were down 2 cartons of cigarettes a piece.

Across the table I caught Fred watching me, giving me that knowing look. It was already understood that if these niggas went too much further they were gonna be down knife money. Meaning whoever didn't pay up got stabbed. Fred and I had already broken the first rule in gambling by allowing the game to be played without the money on the wood. Money out of sight caused a fight. That was one of prison's many colloquialisms. We weren't worried though, because the rules were understood, and nobody at the table had hands free of blood.

Still, it would be incredibly stupid of me to fuck up now considering I only had a couple weeks left before I kicked down the door to freedom. I shook my head at Fred letting him know we would chill for the time being, checking my watch to see how much time I had left.

"You wanna run another one?" I asked Boo Gotti, since I was betting him and Fred was betting Double Oh.

"I thought you had visitors coming today," he replied.

"I do, but you know I'ma always give you a fair shot at your money."

"I dig that, son, but after five games it ain't hard to tell we can't fuck with y'all right now. Let's settle up and we can get down tonight or something."

"Cool," I replied, following him to his cell. Fred went with Double Oh to collect his share of the winnings.

"I got a deal for you," Boo Gotti said once we reached his cell.

Prison was full of deals, dealers, hustlers, con men and thieves, so I was already expecting some type of negotiation. Prison was full of etiquette and unspoken rules, one of which was the only time *you* asked for all your money when you were gambling was if you didn't know the nigga, or you had a problem with the nigga. No currency behind the wall out-weighed a favor. In a lot of ways it was like politics, so me cutting him a deal today would definitely benefit me tomorrow.

"Talk to me, my nigga, what's shaking?" I asked.

"Dig it, let me give you five packs and a box piece of some fire green. You know I got you later."

Moneywise he was only asking for a five-pack break, which was nothing, but it was really a trick because he knew I'd smoke the weed instead of selling it.

16

"I'm wit it," I replied.

"Bet. Throw the blind up," he said, going for his stash while I covered the windows from prying eyes. You never who was watching and who was working.

"You think you gonna hit on the heroin today?" he asked.

"I should, I mean it'll be my last drop before I get out. You already know what it is once I'm on the outside."

"Yeah, I hear you, but don't be like eighty-five percent of these niggas who say that same shit. As soon as mufuckas taste freedom they forget what life is like behind the g-wall."

"Come on, my nigga, you know I ain't even that caliber of dude. My word is definitely my bond, and you should know that with the way we've been doing business the last few months."

"I'm just saying," he replied, handing me what equaled a look out on the heroin I was supposed to have later. A favor for a favor.

"You wanna blow one?" he asked, already rolling a blunt.

"Hold up, let me put these cigarettes in the house," I said grabbing the packs he'd sat on the table.

Our cells were right next to each other so it was easy for me to slide out and right into my spot without too much attention. After putting the cigarettes in my locker I picked up the pack I had open, took one out, and stuffed the weed down inside the pack before putting that in my locker too. That wasn't really my stash spot, that was just me not wanting it out in the open or on me while I was getting high.

Once everything was locked up tight I went back to Boo Gotti's cell just in time to see him fire up the good green. When he passed it to me I passed him a cigarette, taking a seat in the chair by the door. *I ain't paranoid, but I do believe in fast exits when the law comes.*

"Who's in the booth?" he asked.

"Your girl, Ms. G."

"Damn, I need to go holla at ma and see what she's on today."

"You the only mufucka I know that she won't send to the hooskow for pushing up on her."

"It's the Latin thing," he replied, laughing around a cloud of smoke.

Ms. Gurrea was a short, thick, Mexican woman that worked our floor three days a week. You could tell she'd been a bad bitch in her younger days because she wasn't hard to look at now. But she didn't take no type of shit. When I first got here some mufucka got caught jacking off in front of her, and the next thing you know Boo Gotti and some of his goons beat him till he pissed blood. Ever since then they were prison married and Boo could do no wrong.

"When she gonna stop faking and come up off the pussy?" I asked.

"Homie, I don't even know. I mean she be letting me play with it in the stairway sometimes, but it's never enough time to get down to business."

"Enough time? Nigga, you only gonna be good for two strokes!" I replied laughing.

"Fuck you!" We both quit laughing when someone knocked on the door, but we didn't panic.

"Yo?" he called out.

"If Zay's in there tell him Ms. G is looking for him," came a voice.

I lit my cigarette before taking down the blind.

"I'ma holla at you later, bruh," I said.

"Have a good visit," he called out as I slid from his room back to mine.

I dressed quickly in the tan jumpsuit we were forced to wear, making sure I had on a fresh white t-shirt to match my air force ones. Once I took my do-rag off and took a shot of mouthwash I was ready to go out the door.

"Zayvion Miller, you've got a visit," Ms. G said once I'd reached the booth.

"Indeed I do."

"Mmhmm, behave yourself," she said, handing me a pass and my I.D card.

"I wouldn't know how," I said, with a wink and a smile as I made my way downstairs.

Powhatan wasn't a big prison, but there were two sides to it. There's a receiving side for everyone who first comes to prison, where you're classified and given all types of tests for both educational and health purposes. Then there's the general population side, which was for inmates that had already been through the process, and were considered suitable to remain there.

As far as prisons went Powhatan wasn't the worse, it was a medium security level. To put it into perspective, none of the people I played cards with would stay here permanently, but since I only had a probation violation I would've been afforded that option. I preferred my own house though, and two weeks couldn't come soon enough! When I got downstairs I looked at the clock for the first time, and I saw that Carmen was early. We normally tried to time my visits for right at count time, because that gave us a free hour before my time officially started.

The visitation room was small and it only held ten tables, which allowed for fifty people at a time to radiate through. The receiving side of the prison held at least six hundred dudes, so you can imagine how crazy visiting day is. The trick was you could only see immediate family though, which made me all the happier that I had the good sense to marry Carmen before I ended up in this position. It didn't make me being in this situation any better, but it made it bearable.

I still was gonna have to hear her mouth, and the look she was giving me as I came through the door said she had a lot to say. I gave my pass and I.D. to the CO sitting at the table with the visitor's log and turned just in time to catch a hundred mile per hour fastball in the form of my daughter Ariel.

"Daddy!" she screamed, jumping into my arms and hugging me as tight as she could. She was big for a three-year-old, but she would always be my baby girl.

She had her momma's coco brown skin and wild natural hairdo, with my pearly white smile and pug nose. She was beautiful, just like her momma.

"How's my baby?" I asked, carrying her back to the table.

"I miss you," she replied, hitting me.

"I miss you too, Grumpy Bear."

"Then why the fuck haven't you called home all week?" Carmen asked.

I knew this was probably the main reason for her attitude, but I was hoping we didn't have to get into it this quick.

"Damn, can I get a moment with my daughter before you start the shit?" I asked.

"Sure. Just remember who has to console your daughter when she's crying because daddy hasn't called her." I had absolutely no comeback for that. All I could do was hold my baby tighter.

"I'm sorry, babe. I really just didn't feel like arguing with you and somehow that's how all of our conversations turn out."

"That's because you told me this shit wouldn't happen again, Zay. Do you remember that? Do you remember the promises you made me and the quote unquote 'insurance' you had to keep yourself out of prison? I know we kept living life and pushing it to the limit, but prison was never supposed to happen. You convinced me to have a baby with you, and promised to be there for the both of us, but not only are you gone, you don't even call home when you should," she said frustrated.

"Yes, babe, but the parole violation only meant a few months…"

"One day is too long, Zay! Do you know what it's like without you there when I open my eyes in the morning? Do you know how bad my heart hurts when I know all our daughter wants is her daddy, and I can't give her that?"

"Sweetheart, I know how bad you hurt and it kills me that I am hurting our daughter, but I have to swallow those emotions in order to survive in here. I do want to call you and talk to you, but I don't want you to think that I am just being coldhearted when I can't say what it is that I truly feel. These last 5 years have been the best of my life and not just because of Ariel, but because you and I have become one. Waking up next to you every morning and going to do my dirt in the streets, while knowing your love will wash me clean again at night, is what has kept me moving and motivated. Every promise I made I'm gonna keep. I'll be home soon and we'll be good."

"For how long? Trying to rebuild puts you in harm's way again and…"

"Wait, rebuild? What the fuck are you talking about?" I asked confused.

"Have you not talked to Rocko either?" she asked. I noticed an immediate change in her tone, and I didn't like it.

"No, I haven't, why? What happened?"

"Ariel go play with the toys," she said, taking our daughter from my arms and setting her on her feet.

Off to the side there was a play area dedicated to small children a few feet away. I brought Ariel to the enclosure so I could speak frankly with her mother once my baby was out of earshot.

"Three houses were hit, and two shipments of guns too," she said.

"Hit by who?"

"The DEA and the ATF, I think. Rocko didn't give me a lot of details, most of what I know came from the news reports."

"Where did all this go down?"

"The houses were in Stafford, Manassas, and Norfolk, Virginia. The guns were caught in B-more and Philly."

What she said meant absolute devastation had struck. The three houses in question were the main distribution spots for our meth, crack, and heroin, but the guns were still our biggest source of income. This wasn't some random raid. Somebody was running their damn mouth.

"Did Rocko get picked up and questioned?" I asked.

"Not that I know of, but he couldn't make the drop this week. He said he needed to stay out of the way."

While I could understand, this had also put me in a bad spot because there were people depending on me. Shit, if this was as bad as I thought it was I might actually need these next two weeks to grind as hard as possible.

"Can you get someone to do the drop tomorrow?" I asked, looking around to make sure we weren't overheard.

"I took care of it," she replied.

"What?"

"I took care of it. I know you needed…"

"Bitch! You delivered an ounce of heroin and you got my daughter with you?" I asked in a furious whisper.

I normally wouldn't come at her like this, but it was clear that she lost her damn mind, and she needed to know how I felt about it.

"Zay, I…I just thought…"

"No, you didn't think! If something happens to you Ariel is in foster care. Don't you ever take a chance when it comes to our daughter. Ever!"

"I'm sorry, Zay. I understand," she replied softly.

I was so mad I might've punched her in her shit if we were anywhere else. I wasn't one to put my hands on a woman, but this extreme lack of judgment on her part had me feeling like taking a page out of the book Ike Turner. I knew she was only trying to hold me down, but no amount of money was worth anything happening to my daughter.

"What else did Rocko say?" I asked.

"Nothing. He said he'd come see you when he could to talk, but for now he was going underground."

"That's what I want you to do, go underground. I'm not sure what's going on, but I don't like it. Keep your eyes open, and trust no one. No one!"

Aryanna

Chapter Three

It was hard not to let my mind wander and analyze the situation going on in the streets, but I only had two hours and my baby deserved my undivided attention. She was my joy, my reason for being and I loved being in the presence of her innocence. For the first hour we played with the different toys the institution set out for the kids of the visitors. Once she was tired of that we got something to eat and she curled up in my arms for her nap.

It always took my breath away when I watched her sleep. Her chubby face was so angelic and peaceful that it was hard not to feel an overwhelming sense of love and protectiveness. All I wanted was to give her the world, nothing less.

"I miss holding her like this," I whispered.

"She misses it too," Carmen whispered back, scooting her chair closer to both of us.

"I'm sorry, babe."

"I know, Zay. The violation was for something stupid. I mean, even the judge didn't wanna send you to prison. Next time we know to notify everyone before we leave town."

"Right."

"I'm worried though."

"About what, babe?" I asked, actually seeing the fear in her eyes that she was giving voice to.

"Whatever is going on in the streets don't sound good. I don't want you coming home to get caught up in none of it."

"So, what am I supposed to do, turn the whole business over to your brother?"

"We've got plenty of money, Zayvion, why can't we just start over and go legit?"

How did I answer that question? I mean what she was proposing sounded good, but the reality was that we were knee deep in a game that didn't like to let people go. Selling ounces, or pounds, or even fucking with a few keys was cool. But when you got in business with niggas whose shipments came in the tons, you know too much.

Rocko and I may have started in the streets of D.C. and Maryland part-time in the life of crime, but that was a long time ago. I was almost twenty-five, which made me damn near an OG in this game. As long as I was living this lifestyle that was a good thing, but once I stopped I became a liability. Think about it, was it easier to change your whole operation or eliminate those who know too much about that operation? Bullets are cheap, so were trigger men.

"How 'bout we take a vacation when I get home? I mean I know shit is cray out there and there is gonna be a lot of shit I am going to have to address, but you and Ariel will always be my first priority," I said sincerely.

"Do you think your PO is gonna go for that?"

"He should, as long as I'm up front about everything. I'll ask him when he comes next week to bring my reinstatement paperwork."

"That's still only a temporary fix, Zay."

"It's a start."

"You got five minutes left, Miller," a CO said, handing my pass and I.D back.

"Are you gonna call me tonight?" Carmen asked.

"I don't know. Do you want me to?"

"You know the answer to that. I might even be naked when you call, so I can do that thing you like," she replied, smiling mischievously.

I pulled her in close for a thorough kiss, sure to make her panties wet and have her anticipating what she was gonna get in a couple weeks.

"You know I'ma hold you hostage once I get home, don't you?" I asked.

"Promises that you better keep," she replied, grabbing my dick hard before scooping our daughter up.

I couldn't stand at the moment, and it only got worse as I watched her juicy ass sway out of the visiting room. Damn, I loved this woman! I made it through the indecency of having to squat and cough naked, and then back upstairs to my floor where I went straight to the phone. My first call was to Rocko, but I got no answer, so I called my homie, Boy Buddha. Buddha had been slanging weed for me for the past two years, and he was also who Rocko went to when it came time to get a personal sack. Rocko only blew when he was stressed, so I was sure he'd go see Buddha.

"What up?" I asked, once he accepted the call.

"Not shit, bruh, sittin' real still for the moment."

"I heard that. You seen Rock?"

"Yes and no."

That meant he served him, but not directly. That wasn't unusual, that was just Rocko playing it smart, especially if he felt like he was under any kind of surveillance.

"Any messages?" I asked.

"Nah, nothing."

"Cool. Be safe out there and I'll talk to you soon, a'ight?"

"No doubt, my nigga, I got you," he replied hanging up.

I had other calls I wanted to make, but I'd have to wait until I made my pick up tonight. Going to my cell, I went in my locker and grabbed my cigarettes before heading to Fred's room. As usual, his ass was at the card table, this time playing poker with the old heads.

"Yo, Fred, let me holla at you really quick," I said stepping in his cell while he gathered his makeshift poker chips.

"You had a good visit?" he asked, closing the door and putting the blind up.

"Man, shit is crazy right now, bruh," I said, pulling out the weed to roll a blunt.

While I twisted up I told him about the shit that was going down on the streets, giving him a somewhat sanitized version to avoid saying anything that could implicate me later. I fucked with Fred, but you never told anyone all your business, especially not behind the wall. Your closest friend today could be your sworn enemy tomorrow, and anything he knew about you could now be used against you. You had to evaluate everybody you came in contact with as if they were on a need to know basis, and understand that nobody really needed to know.

"Shit sounds wild out there. What you gonna do?" he asked.

There is only so much I can do from this position besides strategize, but I'd be home soon, and then I should be able to put the pieces back together.

"Right now, I'ma try to forget, and we gonna smoke a few blunts. You wit that?"

"Light it and pass, my nigga."

We spent the next hour getting baked and laughing our asses off watching Family Guy on TV, but once the munchies kicked in it was time to roll.

"Ayo, make sure I'm up for pill call tonight, but I ain't going to chow," I said, gathering up my shit.

"I got you."

As soon as I made it in my cell I was in my locker reaching for Doritos and honey buns, ready to smash. My cellmate was still at work, which meant I had the spot to myself and could enjoy some peace and quiet. Before I knew it sleep had pulled me under. My dreams were filled with my little girl's face, but all too soon I felt her slipping away. The sound of the key turning in the lock on my door took me from a dead sleep to Defcon five alert in a matter of seconds, causing me to reach for the banger I kept under my pillow.

Maybe I was a little paranoid, but I've seen too much not to be. I was getting money, but I didn't fuck with a lot of people, so of course that had some niggas feeling some type of way. All too often I'd seen it go down when some niggas ran up in one of these six by nine cells that had a set of bunk beds, two lockers, a sink, a toilet and nowhere to run. So even in my sleep my mind was trained to be ready for whatever.

"Calm down, nigga, it's just me," my celly said coming through the door.

The only benefit I had to being in a two-man cell was that the nigga I had to share the cell with was my actual cousin. You couldn't tell by looking at us that we were family. He had me by at least two inches in height, but I outweighed him by twenty-five pounds. He was light skinned compared to my chocolate brown complexion, and he wore his hair in braids instead of the waves. I kept spinning. He was my mufuckin' ace though, no doubt about it.

"What up, Hambone, how was kitchen duty?" I asked sliding the banger back into safety up under my pillow.

"Man, fuck you and that kitchen. Got me smelling like them mystery meat turkey patties they had for dinner. Why you ain't come to chow?"

"Because I ain't wanna smell like you," I replied, laughing and lighting a cigarette.

"I repeat, fuck you!" he said laughing.

"Yo, Zay, they called pill call," Fred hollered.

"Alright, Fred, I'm coming."

"Everything went good today?" Hambone asked.

"Cuz, it's so much shit going on out there right now."

"Like what?"

I filled him in, not with a sanitized version, but with the all the way live fresh off the presses information about what was going down. We'd grown up together and got down in the streets on several occasions, plus I knew we felt the same way. It was family over everything.

"So, what are you gonna do?" he asked.

"I'ma walk right, listen, and observe once I get out. As for what we do in here, you know we gonna party like rock stars until I leave."

"Damn right! You get some of that green off Gotti?"

"Yeah, it's in the cigarette pack. Do what you do, I gotta go see a girl about a horse," I said, putting on my shoes and passing him the rest of the cigarette.

"Bring her panties back with you," he called out laughing.

He was the only one who knew who my connect was on the inside, and that was only because she'd had to come to the cell one night. Niggas was telling so much it was hard to find a mule these days, so if you were lucky enough to get one you guarded that secret with your life. If a mufucka didn't tell on you he'd definitely try to cut your nuts and do business for himself.

"I'm going to pill call, Ms. G," I said once I got to the gate.

She buzzed me through and handed me a pass. You needed a pass to go anywhere in the building, because if you got caught without one by the wrong dickhead you were looking at an attempted escape. Like a mufucka was really gonna try to escape knowing we were literally sitting in the middle of a farm surrounded by six other institutions! If he tried his hand, that was simply his way of committing suicide.

By the time I got downstairs the line from the pill call window was about twenty inmates deep, which was exactly what I needed, speaking occasionally to dudes I knew, I made my way to the front of the line where the CO was sitting behind a desk next to the entrance to medical.

"What's up, Barnes?" I said to the CO.

"Same shit, Miller, you already know."

"Right. Look I'ma go ahead and get my breathing treatment while I wait on the line to go down."

"Holla at whoever is in here," he replied, waving me into medical.

With it being 8 p.m. I knew there were only two nurses working. I didn't know who was in the window passing out meds, but I knew who'd be waiting on me.

"How you doing, Nurse Hayes?"

"I'm fine, Mr. Miller, are you here for your breathing treatment?"

"Yes, ma'am."

"Follow me," she ordered, coming from behind her desk.

She was a pretty red bone with short brown hair, green eyes and an ass so big it was almost intimidating. She couldn't have been more than five feet five inches, weighing a healthy one hundred and fifty pounds, but you couldn't hide nary a curve, no matter what she wore. In public, she was the college educated, proper girl that was out of your league, but I knew a different side of her. I followed her lead into one of the exam rooms where she closed the door and turned the lock.

"How many were in line?" she asked.

"At least twenty. Who's at the window?"

"Old lady Doris, so we got a good thirty minutes."

"Let's get to the business."

"I was surprised your wife showed up at my house today," she said, pulling down her pants and thong to pull the package out of her pussy.

"It won't happen again."

"Why did it happen at all?"

"Because Rocko couldn't make it. He's laying low for the moment, but she made the move without checking with me."

"Really?" she asked, raising her eyebrow at me, genuinely surprised. "I thought you had her in check."

"Iesha, don't start," I said, taking the package she gave me and slipping it into the pocket I had sewed into the front of my boxers. If I got strip searched, I was fucked, but I could stand a pat down.

"I don't wanna argue," she said, peeling my jumpsuit off my shoulders and pushing it to the floor along with my boxers.

When she grabbed my dick I took her face in my hands and kissed her hard, loving the violence of our tongues as we battled for dominance. Iesha was only twenty-one and she wasn't into making love. She wanted to be fucked. I spun her around, pushing her face down on the exam room table while I smacked her ass with my other hand.

"Do it like you mean it," she taunted.

When I smacked her again it sounded off like a small caliber gun in the little room, but all I had ears for were the moans coming from her mouth. I could feel the need in the tautness of her body and it turned me on.

"What are you waiting for?" she asked.

I ripped her thong from around her legs and shoved it in her mouth. She didn't protest, but instead spread her legs wider to welcome me as I pushed inside her fast and hard. Her pussy was tight and wet, throbbing harder than the beating I was giving as I pounded her harder with each stroke. The way her ass clapped back at me was motivation, making me grab her by her tiny waist and pull while pushing. And she was taking it too, using her arms as leverage to push back while working her pussy muscles to wring my dick dry.

The panties in her mouth were barely containing her screams, yet I still served up punishment with backbreaking strokes that guaranteed she'd always be mine. I felt the eruption start in her toes and so I gave her the long, steady back shots that sent us both over the edge of sanity. I thought my legs might collapse, but when I tried to back away she grabbed my hand.

"W-wait. Leave it in f-for a minute," she panted.

The last thing either of us needed was to be caught in this situation, but I could tell things were changing between us, that this as going beyond business and sex. My dick was still hard inside of her, so I tried something different. Pulling back until I was almost out of her, I pushed back inside her inch by inch as slow as I could. I continued doing that until she suddenly told me to stop. When she stood straight up and turned around there were tears running freely down her face.

"Whoa. What's wrong?" I asked panicked.

"It's just...Zay, I want you to be soft with me like you just were, but I'm scared of how it makes me feel."

"How it makes you feel?"

"Yeah. It's like...I know this started as strictly business a few months ago, but now you're the only nigga I'm fucking. I think about you constantly when I can't see you, and that shit drives me crazy. It wasn't supposed to be like this."

I wasn't sure how to respond, but the crazy thing was I know what she was feeling. I loved Carmen on some next level type shit, but every time I was with Iesha I wondered if there could or should be more.

"All I can tell you is that I get what you're saying and how you're feeling, but I don't know what to do about it." I admitted.

"No, you don't get it, Zayvion."

"Baby, I do, I..."

"You're not listening! Zay, I'm...I'm pregnant."

Aryanna

Chapter Four

"You're what?" I asked, believing I had to have heard her wrong.

"I'm pregnant," she said again pulling her pants up and leaning against the table, wrapping her arms around herself.

"I…I thought you were on birth control?"

"I am. I'm just not good at remembering to take my pills."

Several smartass remarks came to my mind, but I managed to shut them all down before they could pass my lips. I remembered how scared Carmen had been, so I knew that unless I was offering support it might be a good idea not to say shit. I pulled my boxers and jumpsuit back on, trying to figure out what my next move would be. One thing I knew was that Carmen would kill me if she ever found out.

"You probably want me to get rid of it, and…"

"Why would you say that?"

"Because you're married with a child already and this would mess everything up."

"I admit this ain't a situation I wanted to be in, but we're in it. That baby inside you didn't ask to be given life."

"So what are you saying?" she asked, finally looking me in the eyes.

"I'm saying it is your decision, but I don't want you to kill our baby."

"I can't raise a kid by myself, Zay…"

"I got you, slim, you ain't never gotta worry about that."

"Are you sure?"

"Yeah, I'm sure. There are rules though."

"What do you mean?"

"For starters, we're gonna have to find another job for you, because if I'm not here to protect you I don't want you around these niggas."

"You know I can handle myself, boy."

"That ain't the point. One on one you might be good, but if a bunch of niggas come at you…"

"I get what you're saying. Once you're out I'll quit."

"A'ight. Do me a favor and let me see your phone really quick."

"I gotta get it," she said heading for the door.

I used the couple of minutes to myself to try and organize my thoughts because shit had just got real. This was the exact reason I'd never cheated on Carmen before, because getting another bitch pregnant was something she wasn't going for. I'd have to figure all this shit out once I hit the streets. I knew I kept my poker face intact, but when it came to the emotional turmoil I was feeling right now I really didn't know which way I was going to turn. At this point I was just numb and lost.

"We gotta hurry up," she said, coming through the door and handing me the phone.

"I'll be quick," I said, dialing Rocko's number.

"Yo."

"What up, bruh, it's me!" I said, relieved to hear his voice.

"Mannnn."

"I already know, Carmen came to see me today. That's my bad for being out of touch for so long."

"It's all good. When do you get out?"

"Two weeks, and I'm right back with you. You gonna be cool until then?"

"Yeah I'm good."

"A'ight, just lay low, my nigga, and I'll hit you up in a few days."

"Whatever you say, boss."

"You're funny. Love you, bruh."

"You too, my nigga," he replied hanging up.

To somebody listening in on our conversation it would seem casual or even nonchalant, but we both felt the weight of how real shit was. In this game you couldn't cry over spilt milk, so at this point I was only concerned about whether it was about life or death for him out there. Him telling me that he was good meant he was out of harm's way for the moment.

"What's your schedule this week?" I asked, handing her the phone back.

"I'm here until Tuesday."

"A'ight. Have you seen a doctor yet?"

"Yes, today. I'm six weeks pregnant."

"I want you to bring me a cellphone tomorrow, that way I can keep in touch with you even when you're not here."

"I can do that, but you gotta promise me something."

"What's that?"

"You gotta be careful. You get caught selling dope in here and they'll hit you with more time. We need you out there," she replied, rubbing her stomach.

"I got you, baby," I replied, kissing her gently. "I'll see you tomorrow, okay?"

"Okay. Thanks for being so understanding, Zayvion."

I kissed her again quickly and then made my way back to the pill line. The whole time I was standing there waiting to get to the window all I kept thinking was that Carmen was gonna kill me. One thing I knew for damn sure was that I couldn't tell her right now. Knowing how crazy Carmen was she'd try to beat the girl until she had a miscarriage.

I took the two Ibuprofen the nurse gave me, and then made my way back upstairs.

I spotted Hambone as soon as I came through the gate and I gave him the nod so he knew we were on. I trusted no one else to help me piece out my dope, plus he delivered most of it through the kitchen anyway. When I passed Fred at the card table I tapped him on the shoulder so he knew to keep a look out for me, and I told Boo Gotti the same thing before I locked me and Ham in the cell. The building we were in was three floors high with entrances at the front and back. We were on the second floor and there were thirty-six cells holding two inmates a piece.

When I was handling business I always had one person watching the front while the other watched the back, and since my cell was located in the middle of the whole floor I always had enough time to flush the dope. Selling dope in prison was a federal offense, which meant a nigga had to be on his p's and q's unless he wanted them football numbers.

"Let's get this shit over with," I said to Ham, pulling the locker up to the bed so we could both sit on one end and work.

I quickly cleaned off the top of the locker until he ripped up the pieces of paper the dope would go in. We'd break the ounce down gram by gram and move each for four-hundred dollars a piece. I could've charged more, but being greedy inspired more hate than the extra money was worth. A hustler's success was built on balance. It couldn't be all you and no them, just like on the streets when a fiend came to you with seven dollars instead of ten dollars you still gave him a dime bag.

Some of the dudes I dealt with had cash money that they'd snuck in through visitation, but most of my transactions were done with Green Dot cards. It was simple, and the administration couldn't stop it. If a mufucka wanted two grams from me his people would go to the nearest CVS, seven-eleven or Walmart and get a Green Dot credit card, which allowed them to put eight-hundred dollars on a disposable card. I load the money onto my Green Dot card, and just like that the transaction was done.

So, a dude didn't have to get on the phone and talk reckless, all he had to do was get the Green Dot info and he could get as high as his money would take him. Once we had our workspace cleared off and the windows covered up I pulled the dope out and we got down to business.

"You smell like pussy."

"You mad or nah?" I asked smiling.

"Hell yeah! I ain't had no pussy in so long I'm scared my shit won't work right no more."

"Stop being stingy with your money and buy some then, my nigga."

"Man, these bitches are fugly!"

"Oh, my bad, I thought you was just trying to get your dick wet. I didn't know you was looking for a wife."

"Yeah, that's easy for you to say because you got Hayes fine ass."

I chose to let that comment slide and focus on the task at hand. It took money to survive in prison while supporting my family on the street, plus I had a new baby on the way, and so I needed my full attention to be on this grind. With me being in here Carmen was in control of all the money and she was gonna notice any big amounts missing. It might be necessary to make one more drop next weekend. The thing about selling dope behind the wall was the prices, because the supply and demand aspect meant I could charge whatever.

Like Jay-Z said though, I never sold my weight wet, which meant I played fair. Still I needed the inflation the penitentiary sales brought.

"What's on your mind, fam? You got this far off look in your eyes."

"Huh?"

"You moving on autopilot over there in deep thought. I know the pussy ain't got you open like that," he said laughing.

"Nah, I'm focused on this money and the moves that gotta be made."

"That's all, huh?"

"Yeah."

"Cuzzo, I know you," he said, looking at me closely over the pile of heroin between us.

How much should I tell him? I mean if there was anyone I could talk to it was him, but I doubted even he could see a way out of this without somebody's feelings getting hurt. I stopped packaging long enough to roll a piece of paper into the form of a straw. Taking the same playing card, I'd been using to divide up the dope I made a small line for myself, and snorted it.

"That bad, huh?" he asked, getting himself a bump and joining my party.

We only indulged on occasion, and we didn't go anywhere near needles.

"Roll a blunt," I said, trying to find the words that would explain the mess I was in.

By the time I finished bundling up my half of the dope he had the blunt lit and was looking at me expectantly. The heroin had me feeling nice, and suddenly my inhibitions about speaking the truth were lifted.

"She's pregnant."

"Who?"

"Hayes."

"Oh…damn," he replied passing me the blunt.

"My point exactly. Shit is about to get serious, you know how Carmen is."

"So what are you gonna do?" he asked, trying to hold in his laughter.

"I don't know. I'll figure that shit out once I hit the streets."

"Don't worry, I'll look out for her when you leave."

"Yeah whatever, nigga, you're forgetting that I know you too."

"Aww, cuz, what's that supposed to mean."

"It means that me and you ain't about to get into the habit you and my brother share of passing bitches around."

"But it's so much fun," he replied laughing.

"Get it out your head, my nigga. Finish up here, I'ma make these drops really quick," I said passing him the blunt, and grabbing seven grams. I didn't have time to waste, because I could feel myself wanting to nod already.

My first stop was to see Gotti where I traded three for a flat half of the green he had. It was a weed drought at the moment, which meant it was one hundred dollars a gram. But like I said, it was all about favors. Once I was done with him I posted up by the phone and waited for my two white boys to come through with their green dot numbers. I may gamble without seeing the money, but it was very rare that I gave a mufucka my dope without having that money up front.

Once I had both sets of numbers I called Carmen and had her load the sixteen hundred dollars on our card, passed off the dope, and talked to my baby before she went to bed. I knew Carmen was gonna try to have phone sex, but I wasn't on that tonight because my mind was still on Iesha. I stayed on the phone with Ariel until I knew it wasn't enough time for what Carmen wanted, and then I made a deal with her for tomorrow, because the phone line was too long to call back.

I felt bad, but the guilt had to be put away until something could be done about it.

"Everything good?" Fred asked when I got off the phone.

"Yeah, we'll be done in a minute. You want food, cigarettes, or green?" I asked.

"You know I'm good, bruh."

I just looked at him and waited for him to stop playing games. He was my nigga, sure enough, but nothing was free in prison. I never wanted a mufucka to feel like I owed him anything, not even an explanation, so I took care of everybody who rocked with me.

"Let me get some green," he finally said.

"Cool. I'll be at your spot before lockdown."

When I got back to my celly, Hambone was just finishing up packaging.

"How much you moving tomorrow?" I asked.

"I'ma take half with me."

"A'ight, I'ma stash the rest, but send word up if you need more."

I wrapped the remaining fourteen grams in Saran wrap and aluminum foil before I stuffed it down inside my jar of peanut butter. It would all be gone sometime tomorrow anyway, but you never knew if a shake down was coming in the middle of the night, so you had to be ready. Most people had several different stash spots for their dope and their weapons, but the old heads had taught me the value of keeping my shit on me.

The hand was quicker than the eye and shit was easier to get rid of if you had it on hand. Paying off certain COs ensured that I knew when the major shakedowns were coming. Prison was a lot like the streets in terms of how you did business and avoided detection, which explained why street savvy niggas survived and squares became prey. After I had the dope stashed I pinched out a couple of grams for Fred and took them to his house so he could get right for the night.

With business out of the way the only thing left to do was take a shower and go to sleep. I grabbed everything I needed and made my way to the three-stall shower room that was across from my cell, but as soon as I stepped inside I pulled up short. The sight in front of me was disturbing, yet typical, as two black dudes held a smaller white dude down over a chair while a third black dude fucked the shit out of him. I could still hear the white boy grunting in pain, but he knew that if he screamed they would kill him.

"No shower open?" Ham asked when I came back in.

"Not tonight. Don't wake me up for breakfast unless you have to, but I'll come down at lunch to see what's up. And don't smoke all the bud either, nigga," I warned, laying down.

As soon as my head hit the pillow the heroin in my system found its next level and I was riding wave after wave of colors. Sometime during the night, I passed into the land of sleep and there I remained until I heard a banging that wouldn't quit. I opened my eyes to see our day shift floor officer, Ms. Burnette, peeping in my window, and I waved to her to open the door. Most COs would just come in your cell when they felt like it, but some of them had respect.

"You gonna sleep all day, Miller? You ain't been out all morning to speak to me."

"I'm sorry, Burnette, how you doing today?" I asked.

"Shit, still hung over from partying last night."

Burnette was fifty, but she didn't know it yet, and she sure didn't look it. She had long blonde hair that you'd never find a streak of gray in, clear blue eyes, a cute face and a nice body. She knew she looked good and she loved the attention she got, but I fucked with her because she always kept it real with me.

"You have fun last night?" I asked, sitting up slowly.

"From what I remember, yeah," she replied laughing.

"You're crazy."

"Trust me, you have no idea," she said, winking at me.

"Anyway, you've got a legal visit so put your shoes on and meet me at the gate."

"A'ight," I said, grabbing my toothbrush and washcloth.

I knew it was only my PO, but I still couldn't go anywhere with a tart mouth and eye buggers. After making myself presentable, I got my pass from Burnette and headed downstairs to the lawyer meeting room. This would be a good time to talk to him about the vacation Carmen and I wanted to take, because the last thing I wanted was another six months in here for leaving town.

"Mr. Walker," I said extending my hand. I didn't realize there were two other people in the room until the door closed behind me.

"Have a seat, Mr. Miller," my PO instructed.

I did as I was told, but I was studying these other visitors. The woman was about five feet nine inches, one hundred and thirty pounds, average face with brunette hair pulled into a bun so tight I thought I could see her brain moving underneath. The dude was about my height, but I had him by ten pounds at least. He had a buzz cut, a long nose, and scars from his acne. They had one thing in common though. They were undoubtedly cops.

"What's up, Mr. Walker, am I being transferred somewhere? I thought I could sign my reinstatement papers here?"

"Mr. Miller, there's been a slight change. Your probation isn't being reinstated because..."

"We can take it from here, Mr. Walker," the woman said.

"Zayvion Miller, you have the right to remain silent. Anything you say can and will be held against you in the court of law. You have the right to an attorney. If you can't afford one, one will be provided to you by the courts. Do you understand these rights as I have read them to you?" she asked.

"Who the fuck are you?" I asked, trying to maintain my composure.

"DEA, ATF," she replied pointing at first herself and then the other guy.

The feeling in the pit of my stomach told me I wasn't gonna like whatever came next. My probation not being reinstated only meant one thing. I wasn't going home.

Aryanna

Chapter Five

"Do you know why we're here, Mr. Miller?" she asked.

"I still don't know who the fuck you are."

"Forgive me, I'm DEA agent Danielle Brooks, and this is ATF agent Hue Parker." Both of them displayed their badges this time so I could see this wasn't a game. I looked at them, then at my PO, then back to them.

"I'll ask you again, do you know why we're here?"

"Not a clue," I replied.

"You're not a good liar, Mr. Miller," Parker said.

"I'm not lying. I have no idea who you are or why you're here, because I was only expecting my PO"

"Allow me to enlighten you then. About a week ago three major drug houses were raided in different part of Virginia, and a lot of narcotics were confiscated. Agent Parker is here because two shipments of illegal firearms and ammunition were seized in Pennsylvania and Maryland. Do you know what all these incidents have in common?" Brooks asked. I shook my head and waited on the punch line.

"You're what they have in common, Mr. Miller. Everyone we talked to and every tip we got had the name Zayvion Miller in it."

"Yeah, right. Well in case you didn't notice, I'm kinda sitting in prison, and I'm sure my alibi will hold up," I replied smiling.

"Is that a fact?" Parker asked.

"It is. Besides, if you had anything on me, you'd have warrants instead of trying to get me to do your job for you."

"Funny you should mention that," Brooks said, pulling her briefcase from under the table and sitting it in front of her. She popped it open and took a folder out, sliding it to me across the table with a smile.

I didn't want to open it, but I knew I had to do it. Inside the folder were five pieces of paper, each with my name on them. The last two were for trafficking in illegal firearms and ammunition. Reading this shit in black and white put a tightness in my chest that I'd never known. I didn't know if it was a heart attack, but I definitely saw my life flash before my eyes. They were looking to put me under the jail with shit like this, but the icing on the cake came when my PO slid me a piece of paper to add with the stack.

Due to the nature of the offenses and the fact that I'd been officially charged, I was receiving another violation of probation, and I knew he was trying to give me the five years hanging over my head.

"I want a lawyer," I said, knowing that any further conversation would only hurt me.

"That's a good idea, Mr. Miller. You know, normally we say the first to agree to testify will get the softer deal, but since everyone is lining up against you, I don't think you should look for any help," Parker said.

I could taste the bile rising in my throat as I frantically searched every corner of my mind in an attempt to make sense of what was happening. How could this be happening? And how in the hell would I explain it to Carmen?

"Are we done?" I asked, needing to escape that little room before I vomited or started screaming. I feared that if I did either I'd never stop.

"No, we're not done. Not by a long shot. You can go for now though," Brooks said.

I was in a daze as I left the room, walking strictly from memory. The folder I was carrying felt like a life sentence and I had no idea how to get from under it. For them to actually come at me with warrants meant they had a lot more than just ideas about the shit I was doing. Conspiracy wasn't hard to prove, and it carried more time than the actual crime in most situations. To make matters worse, it was all federal, which meant serving whatever the number was day for day.

"You okay, Miller?" Burnette asked me. I didn't even realize I'd made it back upstairs and I was now standing in front of the gate.

"Yeah, I...I'm okay. I just don't feel good," I replied.

"Well, go lay down and just take it easy today. I'll check on you later, honey.

"Okay."

What I was feeling was indescribable, but I had to screw my game face on before I walked through the gate. This was the jungle and the weak animals got picked off without hesitation.

"What up, bruh, you straight?" Fred asked from his seat at the poker table.

"Yeah, I'm good. Just my PO with some paperwork."

"It's almost over, with your short time ass," he said laughing.

I laughed with him even though I didn't feel it. One thing you absolutely never did was talk about open cases or cases where the statute of limitations hadn't expired, because niggas would hop on your case faster than they would a naked bitch who strolled in here. To me, what was in this folder represented the end of everything I know, but to fifty-five percent of the mufuckas around me it meant a new start at life.

So what if they had to step on me on the way down. Who the fuck was I? The sad part was I couldn't identify that fifteen percent who might keep it real, so I had to keep this info quiet. But I had to tell Carmen. Luckily, there wasn't a line for the phone and I hopped on one immediately, hoping she wasn't running the streets.

"Yes?"

"Hey, babe, what's up?"

"I need you to come see me," I said.

"I thought I wasn't coming back until next weekend."

"Nah, I need you to come see me now."

"Zay, I was just about…"

"Carmen! Shut the fuck up and listen to me. You need to get up here now!" I said forcefully.

I knew my tone would catch her off guard, but it would make her pay attention because I didn't normally talk to her like that. Lucky for both of us that visits ran from Friday thru Monday.

"What's wrong, Zayvion?"

"Just get here. No detours. Come straight here and don't bring Ariel."

I hung the phone up before she could ask any more questions, because the odds were better than good that my phone calls were being listened to. I could hear the worry in her voice, but she was gonna have to put her big girl panties on because the road was bout to get rough. If they had warrants for me then Rocko had to be on the run already, but I couldn't call him until I got the cell phone tonight.

Thinking about the cell phone brought Iesha to mind and the baby she was carrying. As a good dude I didn't want to question the baby's paternity, but the nigga in me knew how scandalous women were at times. I didn't feel like this applied to Iesha, and my instincts never failed me before, but only time would tell. How was I gonna tell her about the indictments though? It was just too much to process right now. I made my way to my cell, careful not to make eye contact with anyone, because I didn't want no type of unsolicited conversation. After locking myself in my cell and covering the window, I took some much-needed deep breaths and willed myself not to collapse.

First things first, I needed a blunt. A big one! It took me twenty minutes to roll the mufucka, because my hands wouldn't stop shaking, but I finally got it twisted and lit, and my nerves relaxed slightly. With each toke, I let my mind expand which allowed me to retrace my steps. The first thing I had to do was control what I could control, and that meant getting a pit bull for a lawyer. I needed a mouthpiece to do the talking, because the shit they were saying definitely needed a translator.

Good lawyers didn't come cheap though, but in this moment, I could thank Jay-Z again for his sage advice about chains being cool to cop. But more important were lawyer's fees. They might not know it, but I was ready to battle. Fuck a plea deal. I was gonna box this bitch up and take it to trial! Something else I could control was how I did business, because getting caught up wasn't a good look. No more holding dope overnight, it went out as quick as it came in. It looked like I was gonna be a guest of the state for a little longer, so I was gonna have to make some moves.

The new violation was to make sure I couldn't get out on bond, and since I knew that, it was better to prepare myself mentally to stay a while. I banged on my wall and a few moments later I heard some tapping at my door. I opened the door without looking because I knew it was Boo Gotti.

"What's poppin,' son?"

"Same ole shit. I got a proposition for you, if you can handle it," I said passing him the blunt.

"I'm listening," he replied taking a seat.

"You know I ain't out to get rich, but I got that dope that makes them come back. What if I supplied your homies wholesale and y'all cornered the market?"

"How much dope are you talking?"

"How much can you handle?"

"Let me get with my people and I'll holla back at you. Cool?"

"Cool. A'ight then," he said passing me the blunt back and leaving.

I finished it off and then grabbed my shit for a quick shower. By the time, I'd showered and got fresh clothes on Burnette was at my door with a pass for visitation.

"I'm surprised you're going this late," she said.

"Yeah, it's my fault, because she didn't know I wanted her to come."

"Well, have a good visit, handsome," she said winking.

I grabbed the folder with my warrants in it and tried to figure out what words I was gonna use to keep Carmen from losing her shit. On a basic level, she understood what me and her brother were into, but the consequences never hit home until that gavel banged. The shoulda, coulda, woulda didn't matter. All that mattered was making it through this and hopefully we could do this together. Truthfully, I didn't have the right to ask her to keep putting up with my bullshit, whether it was another woman or my legal troubles. But I loved her, that's what it all came down to for me. If I had nothing I'd still have that same love for her, but I am a man who is flawed at his core. So, I came with a lot of bullshit that she didn't deserve.

When I came in the visitation room I spotted her all the way in the back by the vending machines, and I could feel her nervous energy. I could see the stressed look on her face, which could only mean more bad news. I expected her to be nervous or maybe even suspicious about my demands to come see me, but the way she was looking held a hint of sadness.

"What's wrong?" I asked, pulling her to me and holding her close.

"I talked to Rocko on my way here and he said he won't be around for a while, but he wouldn't give me no details. I'm assuming that's why you called me down here."

It was good to know that my nigga had made it out before the feds had a chance to pounce on him, plus I knew he'd keep shit moving while I was fighting. The bad news was that Carmen hadn't put the pieces of the puzzle together, so she was gonna be blindsided with what I had to tell her.

"Sit down, babe, so we can talk," I said, pulling her chair right next to mine. Carmen was a fighter and she embodied everything I believed a strong black woman to be, so all I could do was be straight with her.

"Listen to me very carefully. I'm about to tell you some shit that's gonna upset you, but I need you to maintain your composure and remember that we're being watched."

"Okay," she replied, visibly bracing herself.

I slid the folder in front of her and watched while she went through page after page. Her expression didn't change after the first cycling through of my warrants, but she immediately started to go through them again, slowly shaking her head.

"Zayvion…Zay, what's all this?"

"I got a visit today from two different federal agents and my PO That's what they brought me."

"No, this has gotta be some type of joke."

"They don't play like that."

"But it don't make no sense, I mean it's impossible because you been in prison." I could hear the edge in her voice, and the tears in her eyes were moments away from falling.

"Baby, listen to me, and try to stay calm. I don't know what's going on, because like you said I've been in here. Obviously people have been throwing my name around, and Rocko's too because he's on the run, but I'ma fight this shit. We are gonna fight this, okay?"

There was no stopping the tears, but she did manage to keep the hysteria under control despite the way she was shaking. Her eyes held so much pain and fear that it broke my heart to look at her, but to look away was cowardly. I could see her struggling for the words to express herself, but I quickly kissed her in an effort to let hope replace the hopelessness of the situation.

"Tell me what we're gonna do," she said, pulling back and searching my face for answers.

"We're gonna fight, babe. We don't never give up or give in."

"But what exactly are we gonna do, Zay?"

"I need a lawyer first and I want you on top of that A.S.A.P. We need an animal though, Carmen, because this is the feds coming after me, and they only come head hunting."

"Will you get a bond?"

"Not as long as I got the violation on me, but hopefully we can get that heard as soon as my original two weeks are up."

"What am I supposed to tell Grumpy Bear? All she talks about is you coming home," she said, her tears falling faster.

"Don't tell her anything right now, because she won't understand. Besides you'll still be coming to see me at least once a week."

"With Rocko on the run, how are you gonna keep doing business? You're looking at a million easy in legal fees, I know I'm only assuming because we never had to fight nothing this serious. But I see those true crime shows on TV and good lawyers don't come cheap."

"I'm working on that, babe, but you can't have anything to do with it. You have to assume that every move you make is being watched and every word you speak is being listened to. I need you to be squeaky clean, and make sure that there's nothing illegal in that house."

"You know better than that, Zay."

"I'ma have a cell phone tonight. I want you to go buy a new burner phone and don't give nobody the number. I'll have someone contact you and get it for me."

"Okay."

"This is serious, and I mean life or death."

"I understand, Zay. Anything you need me to do I'll do, and I'll do it how you tell me to do it."

"Good. For now, I want you to take those warrants home and put them in the safe, because I can't have them here. And get on the lawyer thing A.S.A.P!"

"Okay. I love you so much, baby," she said kissing me with a feverish desperation.

I felt such relief knowing she was on my side ready to do whatever was necessary. It was us against the world. I kissed her again and then insisted she leave, because I wanted a lawyer by the end of the day. With the feds on my ass I didn't have time to waste. I could tell the CO was surprised by how quick my visit ended, which meant I was 'bout to get a thorough search.

Showing my ass to another man wasn't something I'd ever get used to, but it came with the territory. I made it back to my cell in time for the one p.m. count, which gave me an hour of complete silence to strategize my next move. I didn't know whether Ham had sent for me at lunch, but I pulled all the dope out anyway because it was time to get rid of it. The beginnings of a plan were taking shape in my mind, but I'd have to move carefully and quietly for shit to run smooth.

As soon as the doors were unlocked after count I went to my two white boys to see if they had the funds to make a move, big or small. All of it would still spend as far as I was concerned, plus my mission was to dump all the dope before I met up with Hayes so I could make an investment. When dinnertime came, I went to the chow hall with Fred, knowing that he was just as observant as me, so together we didn't miss shit. As soon as Ham saw me he waved me to come behind the service line.

"Why you ain't tell me you were going to visit?" he asked frustrated.

"It was a last-minute thing, fam. Shit got ill today, but we can talk about that later."

"You good?"

"I will be. What's shaken though, how many you need?"

"I need like ten, for real. Mufuckas got money to blow." I took one gram out of the bundle and passed him everything else.

"Make sure that money is right, cuz."

"Come on, man, you know I got this," he replied, going back to work.

I nodded to Fred and we headed back upstairs, watching those that were watching us.

"I gotta holla at you really quick," I said to him when we got back to our floor. Once we were in my cell with the door closed, I decided not to beat around the bush.

"You know I fuck with you real tough, so I'm bout to make you a proposition. There's plenty of money to be had up here, and we haven't even popped into the general population side. Do you got anybody you can go through on that side?"

"Yeah, my uncle is over there. What you trying to do?"

"Move this and we'll talk," I said handing him the last gram I had.

"How much?"

"Bruh, you got sixty-four years. That gram right there represents how you wanna do it. Don't beat yourself."

Chapter Six

To my way of thinking I needed three or four niggas that I could rock with in order to get the type of money it would cost to buy my freedom. That may seem like an easy thing to find considering how overcrowded the prisons were, but most of the mufuckas around me were parasites. The penitentiary operated primarily on the crabs in a barrel theory, which meant it was always a nigga trying to pull you down with him.

Misery loved company. The trick was to know what motivated a person, and you had to be willing to use violence when necessary. And even sometimes when it wasn't necessary, because violence was the one universal thing that every mufucka respected in prison. I knew I could do business with Fred because money motivated him, just like it did on the streets.

He was a hustla. On the flip side you had a nigga like Boo Gotti who was partly motivated by money, but he also loved violence, so at the end of the day he wanted control. Gang bangin' ran a big part of prison and they loved to monopolize on the hustle, but I didn't mind being the man behind the man. My goal was to make between ten and twenty thousand a week, when it was all said and done. There was only one angle left for me to work.

"How you doing, Nurse Hayes?" I asked, walking into medical.

"I'm fine, Mr. Miller, do you need your breathing treatment?"

"Yes ma'am."

"Follow me," she ordered, intentionally switching her hips until I was damn near hypnotized by her big booty.

I'd be lying if I said I didn't wanna dive in it, but business had to be handled, plus I still didn't know how she was gonna react to my legal troubles.

"I wanna suck your dick," she said as soon as we were behind closed doors.

"What?"

"You heard me. I've been thinking about you being in my mouth all day, and I gotta have it," she replied walking towards me.

"Wait, we need to talk first."

"Talk? Baby, I just said I wanna suck your dick and you wanna talk?" she asked, popping buttons on my jumpsuit until she could fit her hand in and grab what she wanted.

"Baby...Iesha, listen to me, it's serious," I said taking a step back.

"It's serious? Ha...have you changed your mind about us? A-about the baby?"

"No, sweetheart, no just listen for a second."

I ran the whole situation down to her from top to bottom, not sugar coating how bad it looked or how bad it could get for me. To my surprise, she took it with a straight face, although I could see the wheels spinning behind the green of her eyes.

"So, what's the plan?" she asked.

"To get a lawyer and try to get from under this shit."

"That's gonna cost."

"Yeah, I know. I need to ask you a favor."

"What's that?"

"Are there any other nurses here that are trying to make some money?"

"Wait, so you not fucking with me anymore?" she asked, clearly hurt.

"Baby, you're pregnant and..."

"And we're talking about the freedom of my child's father. It's no way I'm not in this with you, so you can forget that shit."

"Iesha…"

"Zayvion, I'll bring another bitch that is a nurse here in to help me, but you're not cutting me out of shit. So let's talk about something else."

Her eyes burned with determination, showing me a side of her that I'd never seen before. I have to admit I liked it.

"Okay, so what do you have in mind?"

"I'ma turn my girl, Trish, onto one of your dudes, but as long as you're supplying the dope is a sixty-forty split."

"We need to start off with two drops a week."

"I'll talk to her tomorrow. Who are you hooking her up with?"

"My cousin Hambone."

"Hold up, you want me to put a bitch up with a nigga named Hambone?" she asked laughing.

"Shut up, it's about business," I said trying not to laugh.

"Okay, whatever you say. What else do you need me to do?"

"I need you to be careful."

"I will…let me ask you something. I'm assuming the DEA and the ATF are just waiting on the indictment to come down. Won't that have a list of all the people set to testify against you?"

"I mean it should, or my lawyer should be able to get it as part of my discovery. Why?" She didn't answer at first, but she stared at me like she was looking for something.

"Say something," I said, pulling her towards me.

"We need to get to know each other better," she said, taking a phone from her pocket and handing it to me.

I put it in my pocket, still unsure of what exactly was on her satellite, but I figured she'd tell me in her own time.

"I don't have a problem getting to know you, but why do you feel like that's important now?"

"Because we're at a new beginning, and we're gonna be a part of each other's lives indefinitely. Don't you wanna know who you're fucking with?"

The way she asked that gave me the chills, but it turned me on too.

"I think I know who I'm fucking with, but I'll gladly learn more."

"Here's your first lesson, when I want something I get it."

I didn't have time to protest before she pulled my dick out and was on her knees kissing it softly. Within seconds I found out she didn't have a gag reflex, and her technique had my knees knocking like the FBI.

"N-not so fast, babe," I mumbled.

But she ignored me. I watched my dick disappear between her succulent lips faster and faster while she used her hand to massage my balls. I was doing my best to hold my composure until she ran her tongue ring from the base of my shaft up to the head of my dick. I exploded so hard my knees finally buckled and I had to lean on her for support.

"I have n-no idea who you are," I panted, wondering how long I'd be seeing stars.

"I'm the woman who just swallowed every drop of your cum, which means for the time being I own this dick, understand?"

"Uh huh."

"Good. I'ma take my break at about midnight so make sure you're up so we can talk. Oh, here take the charger too." I put it in my pocket with the phone and fixed my clothing.

"You know we gotta be careful, right?" I asked.

"Yeah, I know. I just need you to trust me to handle my end."

"What about Carmen?"

"What about her?" I asked immediately defensive.

"What's her role?"

"She doesn't have one, because they're probably watching her."

"True. It's cool. I got you on whatever you need. You need to go though."

I kissed her quickly and left, feeling better than I thought I would. She took the news like a champ. I'd expected crying and some more shit, given the fact that she was pregnant, and it looked like she might be a single mom. I was genuinely surprised, but our relationship had existed on the planes of business and sex so that was all I'd had to go on. Shit was different now, but I found myself looking forward to the change. It felt good to have someone literally in the trenches with me. Carmen was my ace, she held me down accordingly like any wife would, but it was a different feeling when you actually had someone inside the prison with you. When it came to Carmen I had to explain the day to day in here, but Iesha got to see it through her own eyes. Which in turn created a different type of bond and understanding.

It took me a week before I brought my plans full circle, but everything came together nicely.

Fred's uncle was a nigga named Twin, who was an OG for forty-three gangsta Crips, and they ran the general population with an iron fist. I dreaded to start him off with an ounce once Fred came back and told me that he'd made five hundred dollars off the gram I gave him. He'd tried to give me the money, but I made him keep it so he'd understand that we all could eat off the same plate. Twin stood to make an easy fourteen thousand dollars, so we agreed on a nine-five split.

At two drops a week that meant I was scooping up eighteen thousand dollars without having to go through the hassle of slanging the work myself. I wasn't in this for grocery money. I needed that real bread to get ahead. Thanks to Iesha I was able to double down on getting the dope work in, because she put Hambone on with this cute white girl named Trish. Trish had a family to support so she didn't mind bringing that dope in and getting paid for it. It was a risky move, but her willingness to grind meant she needed that money in a major way.

The dope she was bringing in supplied Boo Gotti, and we still did business with a few dudes who preferred to keep their business out of the street. Boo got his ounces for seventy-five hundred dollars, which totaled out to fifteen thousand dollars a week, and I got nine thousand dollars of that. I didn't just get to put this money to the side for my lawyer though, because I still had Carmen and Ariel to take care of, plus Iesha and the baby we had coming.

When it came to Carmen, I just gave her enough where she wouldn't have to dip into our savings right now. Luckily, the house was in her late mother's name and it was paid off, because the feds had intentions on seizing what they could. The smartest thing I'd ever done was keep my wife's hands clean in anticipation of times like this, which is what allowed her to drop twenty thousand dollars cash to retain my lawyer. Anybody can pay for a lawyer, but if you pay for them in cash, which ultimately would have to be reported to the government, you can come under close scrutiny and that meant you couldn't have any skeletons in your closet.

Charles Swedish was an absolute go-getter when it came to fed cases, and I was gonna make sure he earned every dime of his money. Outside of all that though I still had to pay my way inside the penitentiary if I wanted to stay in business. I'd had to buy a hearings officer, a gang investigator, and someone that worked internal affairs, because the last thing I needed or wanted was any type of surprises. I gave Rocko a lot of credit for being the brains behind the operation, but I'd damn sure been paying attention. Despite their gun shipment being seized, the dudes I dealt with in B-More fucked with me so hard that they didn't hesitate to front me dope.

And since I never put all my eggs in one basket I was still able to get them guns from my connect at Boiling ATB in D.C. Every night before we got off the phone I made sure to tell Iesha just how much of a life saver she really was because that cell phone allowed me to minimize the damage done by the feds. It allowed me to get to know her better too. We laughed and joked, but we also had serious conversations about what we wanted for our child's future. Our own childhoods were discussed, along with relationship regrets and ultimately what we wanted or hoped the future might look like.

It seemed like it happened overnight, but before I knew it she and I were actually friends. The danger in that was that neither of us were strong enough to say no to more. In the beginning sex had been a seduction to get her to the point of doing whatever was necessary. It was more now. It was different. As the first week moved into the second and the original day for my release drew closer, I noticed how our time together changed. We weren't on the point of making love, but we weren't just fucking either.

The night I ate her pussy I knew shit was real and so did she, because it brought her to tears. I'd never eaten any other woman except Carmen, and I prided myself on that, but I wanted to taste her. I'd needed to. The night before I was scheduled to be released I spent our entire time together with her riding my face and cummin' in waves of euphoria when she asked me why I told her I wanted no regrets. Tomorrow the world would change. Might even change for the worst.

Aryanna

Chapter Seven

"Do you understand the charges that have been read to you, Mr. Miller?"

"Yes, Your Honor."

"And were you given a copy of the indictments?"

"I was, Your Honor."

"Mr. Swedish, is there a request on the bail amount?"

"Uh, Judge Malloy, the people ask for no bond since Mr. Miller has had his probation violated this morning and is remanded to the state of Virginia's custody."

"Judge Malloy, as Ms. Watkins has already been informed we intend to fight the violation, because it seems premature given the fact that this case has not reached its conclusion."

"Your Honor, either way the charges Mr. Miller faces are too serious to allow him the opportunity to make bond and flee."

"Your Honor, my client has never been a flight risk and..."

"Enough, both of you. Mr. Swedish, I'm inclined to agree with DA Watkins with regards to the probation violation. However, if you're able to get the violation lifted I will allow for a bond hearing. I'm setting the preliminary hearing for six weeks from today, which is July twenty-third at nine a.m. Court is adjourned until then," she said with a swift bang of the gavel.

The screen went blank, leaving just me and my lawyer in the small legal visitation room. It seemed like yesterday that my PO and those agents were here to fuck up my world and from the look of things, it wasn't getting any better. I'd never been to court via TV screen, but the high dollar feds didn't transport for something as small as an arraignment.

"How confident are you that you can get this violation lifted?" I asked my lawyer.

"It depends on a lot of things. It would've looked better to already have a bond set because I could spin it as them not having confidence in their case. As it stands now, I think we've got a thirty percent chance."

"Damn, why so low?"

"Because these charges are serious and there are ten people set to testify against you. Eleven if you count the CI"

"Why is the CI's name not listed?" I asked looking at my indictment for the millionth time.

"Because that part of the indictment is sealed. I don't know who it is, but whoever it is must be a major part of their case against you. Do you have any idea who it could be?"

I've been asking myself the same question since I got a copy of the damn indictment. I didn't recognize some of the names on paper, let alone guessed who was behind door number two.

"I don't know. I mean, I didn't even see this coming."

"Yeah, most of you never do. How many people on this list do you know?"

"I know Michael Clark, James Booth, Timothy Williams, Kristen Jackson, Leon Winton and Jason Sharp."

"How do you know them?"

"I did time with Michael, Tim, Leon and Jason. I used to fuck Kristen and James was my weed guy for a while."

"Did you commit any of the listed crimes with these people?"

"Fuck no! I don't trust none of them to wash my car, let alone do anything illegal. Not one of them mufuckas could the stand pressure, which is obvious," I replied disgusted.

Just a bunch of bitch ass niggas that hated they never made it, and now they were trying to make that my problem.

"And these other four names, Hubert Nelson, Hannah Holland, Jerome Johnson and Derrick Williams, you have no idea who they are?"

"No."

"Okay, I'm gonna put a private investigator on this to see what I can dig up on everyone. I've got six weeks to dismantle everyone's credibility. In the meantime, you need to lay low and come up with a list of character witnesses on your behalf. The one thing you have going for you is that you weren't previously charged with any kind of weapons related or drug offenses. The ass whooping you delivered to get on probation doesn't look good, because it shows you're capable of violence, but to only have one previous conviction is still a plus. It's a real stretch of the imagination to go from a fight to a king pin."

"Can you convince the jury of that?" I asked.

"That's what you pay me for. Speaking of which, I'll need my next installment before the preliminary and then we will discuss the fee for the trial."

"You'll have your money within twenty-four hours," I assured him.

"I'll see you soon," he said extending his hand.

"Make sure my wife gets my copy of the indictment, you know it's not safe to have in here," I replied, shaking his hand and giving him my paperwork.

"Will do."

Once he was gone I took a few minutes to organize my thoughts and get my game face on. I'd lied for as long as I could, desperate to keep my indictments a secret, but I knew there would be questions when I didn't walk out the gates to the open arms of freedom. So far luck had been on my side, because my lawyer had been able to keep my name out of the news and newspaper, plus I'd laid the groundwork for the story of my PO refusing to reinstate my probation.

Now all I had to do was sell it. On my way back upstairs, I noticed quite a few mufuckas nodding or scratching, but the biggest difference was the noise level. Prison was a loud place by nature, but heroin was a downer and as long as mufuckas were high it would be quiet. The COs weren't really interested in why inmates were quiet, they just enjoyed the infrequent moment.

"What's the word, bruh?" Fred asked as soon as I hit the floor.

"The bitch ass judge agreed with my PO to serve me out, but my lawyer is already working on the appeal."

"Yo, I ain't never heard of them doing no shit like that," Double Oh said.

"Welcome to the Commonwealth of Virginia," I replied.

"And that's why I can't wait to get back home, son. At least if we were upstate we'd get them conjugal visits, nah mean?"

"Hell yeah!" Boo Gotti chimed in.

"It is what it is, I'm built to do a bid. My question is are you niggas ready to lose some more money?"

"Spades takes too long, hop in on the poker game," Leslie said.

It was an unspoken rule that gay men, or punks as they were referred to, ran the penitentiary. The administration was too fearful of a hate crime lawsuit that they let the punks get away with anything almost, and in return the punks kept them up to speed. They gossiped more than bitches on the street, and for this reason it was better to be on their side than on the outside looking in. Leslie was an old-school punk, no longer in the game of using his body to get what he wanted because he was sick, but he still proved useful because he'd been down so long.

And he wasn't above sucking a dick if he thought you were cute. Being that Leslie was on my floor, I felt like it was my job to keep him content because I didn't need no drama, especially not right now.

"I'm in Les, but only if you're cooking tonight," I said laughing.

"That is too true, child. What do you wanna eat?" Leslie asked.

"I'm feeling like pizza. I can send word down to Ham to bring up some green peppers and onions."

"I got sausage and pepperoni," Fred offered.

"And who's paying for my services?" Leslie asked.

"I can't believe you would insult me like that, slim," I replied dramatically.

"Pull up a chair, fool ass man, you know I'll cook for you."

I wasn't really good at poker. I mainly used it to pass time. With me, Fred, Boo, Leslie and dude named Jason, that we called white chocolate, I knew no one was here looking to get rich. Some niggas lived off their ability to gamble, and you didn't wanna get locked into a game with them unless you were just as serious. I just wanted a few hours to take my mind off of everything. I ended up playing until shift changed and Ms. G hit the floor, and I even won twenty dollars, but I gave it all to Leslie.

Every CO that worked in prison wasn't cool with looking the other way and they couldn't be bought. That meant I had to move accordingly and keep my head down so it wouldn't get knocked off. Tonight was the night Boo Gotti was supposed to make his move on Ms. G., so once she came in we stepped away from the table.

"Are you sure about this?" he asked once we were in his cell.

"I'm positive, my nigga, trust me. You're not asking her for shit, all you're doing is showing her that you care about her. This is how you lay the foundation for the long con," I said passing him five hundred dollars in cash.

The idea was for him to give her the money, no strings attached. Of course, she was gonna call bullshit, but if he did like I told him and just got her used to the idea of him giving without expecting shit it would make her wanna do things for him. It would take time and money, but it was as worthy an investment as blue chip stock on Wall Street.

"You got this, my nigga, just handle your business."

I gave him the money and went to make sure the man took my message to Ham about the food. When I got back in my cell I got my phone out of its hiding place in the wall and saw that I had seven missed calls from Carmen. I couldn't call her back now, but the trick to having a phone was to look like you didn't have a phone. That meant keeping up appearances by using the phone in the unit.

I sent her a text letting her know I was about to call from the recorded phone so she wouldn't say anything stupid. She knew the trick to talking without talking, but I wasn't taking any chances by not warning her. I plugged my phone into its charger and hid it under my pillow, locking my door on the way out, and got in line to make my call.

"I'm about to start cooking in a minute. Do you want me to make a cake?" Leslie asked.

"You got the cookies for all that?"

"Yeah, plus I figured I'd do that first since Ham doesn't get off for another hour."

"That's cool. Hey…how are you feeling today?" I asked, careful to keep my voice down so others wouldn't overhear.

Everybody knew Leslie was sick. I mean AIDS ain't really something you can hide when it gets to that full-blown stage. Growing up I watched a few of my close family members lose their battle with the disease. Subconsciously maybe that was why I dealt with Leslie the way that I did. On bad days, I would give him something to ease the pain, and he knew if the day ever dawned that he was done fighting I'd send him out sky high. I didn't care how many agreed with me, they weren't the ones dying in pain every day.

"I'm good. I thought I was coming down with a cold, but I'm alright."

I could see the fear in his eyes, because he knew as well as I did that it wasn't AIDS that killed you. It was the breaking down of the immune system to the point that a common cold could kill you.

"Do you need anything?" I asked.

"No."

"Leslie?"

"Zay, I'm fine. You know I'd tell you if I wasn't."

"A'ight. Make sure you put your foot in that cake."

"You know how I do it," he replied smiling.

It was my turn on the phone and I dialed Carmen's number quickly. I didn't get a chance to say hello good before she was asking me what happened in court. I told her how it went down and that my lawyer would be to see her with my paperwork. She was curious about the sealed part of the indictment, but she was determined to keep her ear to the street for any loose gossip. Arguing with her to stay out of the streets was useless, but I knew nine times out of ten she was gonna have Rocko listening, since he was still plugged in.

We talked about our upcoming visit and she put me on notice that Ariel would only be with her on one of the days because we need alone time together. I couldn't lie, despite how close Iesha and I had gotten I still missed my wife like crazy. I spent the rest of my call talking with my baby girl, and we hung up just in time for me to see the smile on Ms. G's face when she finished making her rounds on the floor and headed back into the booth. Boo Gotti appeared from his cell with his swag on full tilt, and it looked like a plan was coming together.

I decided to kick back and watch TV for the rest of the evening, only leaving my cell when Ham came in to get himself together after his shower, and when I was summoned by the king of queens to get my pizza and cake. It wasn't home cooking, but to be able to share a meal with people I fucked with still went a long way at making me feel somewhat human. Even though Leslie didn't ask for it, I still slid him half a gram on my pill call. I was looking forward to seeing Iesha, and I'd been feeling that way a lot lately, but when I got downstairs there was a bunch of commotion. She didn't even waste time with the normal rhetoric, she just told me to follow her to the back.

"We've gotta take one to outside medical due to stab wounds, so we can't do anything tonight," she said, clearly frustrated.

"It's okay, babe, we can still talk later on."

"Did you have court today?"

"Yeah, I got indicted and the violation, but my lawyer is on his shit."

"Did they release the names of the people snitchin' on you?"

"All except one. There's a CI and that part of the indictment is sealed."

"Okay, I want you to write everyone's name down," she said, handing me a pen and piece of paper.

"Why, babe?" I asked.

"I need you to trust me, Zay. I've got somebody who's gonna investigate."

I'd never heard of having too many investigators, plus street niggas would always get more results than someone with a badge. I wrote down everyone's name and gave it to her.

"Thanks, babe. I'ma call you later," she said, giving me a toe-popping kiss that had me ready to rip her uniform off.

Back upstairs I rolled a blunt and kicked back, saddened that I wasn't home, but happy another day was behind me. When it came to doing time, it was better to be grateful than bitter, because tomorrow wasn't promised, and neither was freedom. I dozed off watching a movie on BET, but the vibration of my phone woke me up at a little past two a.m. It wasn't a call. It was a text message with a picture. I recognized the person in the photo, but the bullet hole in her head wasn't there when I last saw her. Kristen was definitely dead and the message was simple. No more talking.

Aryanna

Chapter Eight

"Damn, you're beautiful," I said, admiring the way her blue summer dress complimented every curve on her body.

"I'm glad you still think so," she replied, kissing me with that hunger I'd been missing for a while now.

"Carmen, you'll always be beautiful to me. What are you talking about?"

"I don't know. I just don't feel that way a lot anymore because I don't have you around to show me everyday...I really miss you."

"I miss you too, baby, every moment we're apart. And I know that you know you're a bad bitch, so don't ever doubt yourself. I'll be home in a minute to show you."

"Do you promise?"

"Of course, I do."

"How can you promise me that, Zayvion? I read your indictment, plus I talked to my brother, so I know how serious it is. Rocko doesn't exaggerate things, but he's even worried about me visiting you right now!"

"That's just him being extremely paranoid, and over protective. Baby, everything is gonna be fine," I said, hoping to reassure her.

I knew she heard me despite the fact that she'd suddenly found interest in the unseen depths of her soda can. I didn't wanna spend our whole visit trying to convince her that everything was alright, but I could read the fear in her body language. I knew Rocko was just trying to mentally prepare her for the worst-case scenario, but I was gonna have to tell him to chill on the scared straight tactics.

"Carmen, look at me. Have I ever broken a promise to you, baby?"

"No."

"So, will you please have a little faith in your man?"

"I'm trying," she said, visibly fighting the tears that were beggin' to be shed.

I hated to see her in so much pain and turmoil, but there was only so much I could tell her right now. Being honest with myself, I could admit that this whole situation was on the verge of getting out of hand quickly.

I hadn't seen Iesha in three days because she'd been off, but even if I could've seen her, I didn't know that I would. I didn't expect her to somehow just start knocking mufuckas off once I told her who was on my case, but apparently, I'd underestimated her willingness to keep me free.

I respected a loyal person, but I felt like she could've gave me a heads up. Her reasoning had been plausible deniability. They were permanently removed from the witness list, but there was no way I could tell Carmen what was going on. She was just gonna have to trust me when I said I'd get from under this. I mean I did still have my emergency plan in the back of my mind.

"Is it hard to wait for me?"

"Zayvion, why would you say some shit like that? There ain't no other nigga out here I'm checking for. I'd wait forever for you."

"I know that, babe, I'm just asking if it's hard for you."

"Not in the aspect of just missing a man. I miss my husband and what used to be a normal life we shared together. I miss watching you play with Grumpy Bear, because I swear there's never been a bigger daddy's girl. So yes, it's hard, but only because I didn't think we'd be in this situation, and you assured me that we wouldn't be."

There was heavy blame in that last statement, but I deserved it. I'd promised her a certain life and so far, I wasn't delivering.

"Sweetheart, listen to me, I know shit ain't the way we planned, but no matter what happens I want you to always remember these words. I got you. Hear me?"

She took her time responding and I could see the contemplation in her eyes, but at the end of the day we'd been through too much to turn back now. The slight smile she was giving me indicated she felt the same way.

"I hear you...I've got three words for you, too. No panties on," she replied, smiling wickedly.

"Hold that thought," I said, getting up and going to have a word with the CO working visitation.

Graves worked visitation on the regular and we already had a standing arrangement that I paid for monthly, and it was worth every cent.

"How much time we got today?" I asked.

"It's crowded, so I'd say ten minutes."

"Shit you won't last that long," she replied laughing.

I was gonna do my best to make her pay for that comment when the time came. Having sex with my wife in the prison bathroom wasn't ideal, but we had to do what we had to do. The sweet thing about this visitation room was there were three bathrooms, one for men, one for women and one for inmates. The one for inmates was conveniently tucked in the corner, almost out of range of the camera angles. The cameras didn't matter though, because when you paid a CO he would have whomever was behind the camera focused in another direction when we went in and come out. All I had to do now was wait on the signal.

"Why are you looking at me like that?" she asked.

"Like what, babe?"

"Like you're about to fuck me up or something."

"Well, you did kinda challenge me, didn't you?"

"Zay, I was just joking. You know how long it's been, because we thought you were coming home. You gotta be gentle with me." Hearing those words come from her lips made me laugh, but before I could respond I caught the nod from Graves.

"It's time," I said, getting up and going to the inmate bathroom.

As soon as I closed the door I started counting, knowing that when I reached thirty seconds she would be coming through the door. There wasn't a moment to waste, so I was already pulling my jumpsuit and boxers down, stroking my dick while I was counting the seconds.

"Baby, please," she whispered once she was inside with the door firmly shut behind her.

"Shhh, come here," I demanded, pushing her dress up to her waist and sticking my middle finger in her pussy while my thumb rubbed her clit.

"Mmm, you're super tight."

"That's why you have to be gentle."

My kiss was the exact opposite of that as my mouth explored hers in a barely contained fury. My aggressiveness took her breath away, but I could feel the electricity of passion coursing through her body as I backed her into the wall and took her off her feet. Her legs wrapped around my waist of their own accord when I plunged into her, while her screams ran down my throat like we were breathing as one.

I could feel her trying to relax, but my onslaught of strokes was giving her life, something she couldn't deny she needed. We took turns biting each other's lips, drawing blood in an effort to stifle the sounds of the animal within. Still I pounded her tight pussy like I was aiming to drive her through the concrete wall. When she came the first time it was a sudden opening of the floodgates and I could feel her nails digging into me through my t-shirt. Turning from the wall, I sat her on top of the sink, not missing a stroke while pushing her back and wrapping my hand around her throat.

Her eyes bulged and burned with desire as I gave her the long dick, tickle your ribs, type of punishment, while choking off her screams before they could reach the visitors on the other side of the door. It felt so good to be inside her that I lost myself and before I knew it we were cumming together, exchanging beautiful fuck faces and breathless I love yous.

"That-that h-hurt so good," she panted, gently getting down off of the sink.

"I'm glad. You know what I want you to do now though?"

"Mmm tell me," she purred.

I stepped out of my clothing so I was just wearing my sneakers, socks and t-shirt, and then I stood on the toilet.

"You got my dick dirty, now clean it off."

She stepped up and took all of me in her mouth in one gobble, making sure to look up at me as she slowly worked me back and forth. Nobody gave dome like Carmen, and she had me weak kneed before she took my dick in her hand while she sucked my balls. I heard the microwave beeping which meant our time was up, but now she was a woman on a mission and I was along for the ride.

"B-baby, we gotta... Awww!"

"You were saying?" she asked licking her lips and pulling her dress back down.

I stood there speechless as she laughed and made a fast exit. It took me a few minutes to gather my composure and got dressed, but I eventually made it back to the table where I found my wife still smiling.

"You almost killed me," I whispered.

"Like you weren't trying to kill me? Nigga, I tasted blood when I had you deep in my throat."

"What you mean?"

"I mean you fucked the shit out of me!" she whispered laughing.

"Bet you won't challenge me again."

"I might. It was definitely worth it, and we need that type of action if it's gonna work."

"If what's gonna work?" I asked.

"If we're gonna work. Baby, I know you and I know your sexual appetite and I'll be damned if I lose you to some bitch in here because you ain't out to get what you need. I understand that sex ain't better than love, but I want to be the only woman you're getting both from. So, I'm gonna put this pussy on you whenever possible."

"Carmen, you are my wife and you should know by now that you're the only woman that got what I need. No matter how long I'm locked up it will be you I turn to for comfort. We are facing forever together no matter what happens. It's us against the world, do you understand?" I asked kissing her quickly on the lips hoping she didn't see right through me.

There was no doubt in my mind or heart about the love I had for her. In a perfect world she'd be my one and only. This world wasn't perfect and I damn sure wasn't, however I loved her enough to tell a pretty lie instead of the ugly truth.

"I understand it's us forever, baby, and nothing or no one will come in between that," she replied taking my hand into hers.

The remainder of our visit was used discussing our daughter, future visits, and what life would look like when this chapter was behind us. All I could do was continue to pray that she didn't find out about Iesha, because all of the plans we were making would vanish.

When I got back to my floor I saw Hambone standing outside our cell with the door wide open, which could only mean one thing. Shakedown.

The CO had the option to dismantle your cell at any moment throughout the day. Some did it because they really expected to find something, some just wanted to be assholes. Ham and I locked eyes, but I didn't see any worry in his, which indicated that they hadn't found anything, and they probably wouldn't. The two COs doing shakedown were Timothy and Capel.

Timothy was an asshole, and he couldn't be bought, which meant you had to tolerate him or end up in the hole, after you got your ass whooped. On more than one occasion I'd heard him tell a mufucka that he'd never lost a fight to a nigga in handcuffs. His partner in crime was a CO named Capel. He wasn't as bad as Timothy, but he thought he was some type of player/pretty boy with the three golds he had in his mouth and the small ass gold rope he wore around his neck. Capel's main focus was fucking every new female CO that came through the door. But he went along with Timothy's bullshit for shits and grins.

"You find what you were looking for?" I asked from the doorway.

"Well, well, look who decided to join the party," Capel said.

"What up, Capel?" I asked.

"Just living the dream."

"Anything in here we should know about?" Timothy asked.

"Is that a serious question?" I replied.

"Just trying to give you a chance before I started breaking shit," he said smiling.

"Make sure you write down anything you destroy so they can dock it from your pay. I've got receipts for everything."

"I bet you do," Capel said.

"Miller, you need to go to medical!" Burnette yelled from the gate.

"Watch them, cuz, I hear a CO's pay ain't shit, so their fingers might get sticky," I said, walking away.

I could hear Capel laughing. I got my pass and headed downstairs trying to figure out what I was going to medical for. It was too early for Iesha to be here, and the doctor didn't work on the weekends.

"What's up, Davis?" I asked the female CO sitting behind the desk next to medical.

She reminded me of a bitch you would call Boss Hogg: short and fat with all the facial characteristics of a pig. She was cool though unless you disrespected her.

"I ain't doing shit, Miller, just maintaining."

"Why am I down here?"

"I don't know. Hayes said she needed to check your flow chart before your breathing treatment tonight so the dosage would be right."

In my mind, I was saying what the fuck was she doing here early, but all I did was shake my head and went into medical. I spotted her at the end of the hall and she waved me to come to her.

"You're early," I said closing the door.

"Yeah, I know. I ain't seen you in three days and I came to spend time with you. But you were at a visit with your wife."

The tone of jealousy was so blatant that I couldn't miss it if I tried.

"Iesha, maybe we should get something straight. Carmen is my wife and that ain't changing. Do I have feelings for you, of course, and you should know this. But you knew what it was when we started this."

"Yeah, I did. I didn't expect to be falling for you or for us...."

"Wait, wait, pause. You're what?"

"You heard me, Zayvion, but we can deal with that when the time comes. Right now, we got a problem."

"What's that?" I asked.

"Capel."

"What about Capel?"

"Before you and I started kicking it, I went out with him a couple of times, but it wasn't nothing serious. And before you say some shit that'll get you cut, I have no problem giving you a DNA test once the baby is here."

"I wasn't gonna go there, slim. Explain to me what the issue is."

"This nigga won't leave me alone! He keeps blowin' my phone up and coming to my house unwanted. Now he's talking 'bout getting me fired."

That statement alone meant this shit was beyond a problem, because now was not the time to fuck up the way we were moving.

"What do you wanna do?" I asked.

"I want it fixed. Permanently."

Aryanna

Chapter Nine

Permanently? The word echoed through my mind louder than a gunshot in a project hallway. I could admit that this nigga was a problem, because him pressuring Iesha in any way stressing her was unacceptable, but I wasn't sure death was the only solution. Prison had many faces and officers getting fucked up or killed was definitely one of them, but the heat that came with a move like that was inescapable.

"Permanently," I repeated.

"I'm sorry, is that too real for you? Some nigga is threatening your baby momma and you wanna have a conversation or something? I'm not good enough to be protected? I…"

"Hold up and slow the fuck down. Damn! I didn't say none of that, so don't put any words in my mouth. But since you got so much to say, how do you suggest we go about this permanent solution?"

"I mean you know people in here so I figured you could get it taken care of," she replied.

That sounded good, but it didn't ring true. She was the one getting mufuckas lights turned out in the streets, which meant she definitely knew some shady characters. Why bring it to me? Why, when she knew a murder charge in prison would cost me my life? The answer was simple for a nigga from the streets. I was being tested. Iesha knew I was 'bout my money, but the question of whether or not I'd get blood on my hands was a mystery to her. Maybe she wanted to know, or maybe whoever had put that work in on my behalf wanted to know. Either way, it was a test. Most mufuckas didn't understand that violence wasn't supposed to be a reckless thing you engaged in off of emotions.

It was a tool you used in a calculated fashion in order for its effects to be maximized. Anything worth doing was worth doing right. The fact that she brought this situation to me the way that she did told me that I was dealing with a bitch of young minded people. What that meant was if I knew this and still let them out think me then I deserved whatever I got for that mistake.

"I can take care of it. I just need some information on him." I said.

"Like what?"

"What he drives, where he lives. Does he have any kids, what he does away from work?"

"What are you gonna do?"

"I'm gonna make the problem go away."

"How?"

"You're asking too many questions. Just get me the info I need."

"I'll get it. Here," she said, passing me a condom that had an ounce of weed in it out of her bra.

"What the fuck are you doing walking around like that?"

"Chill, I wasn't the one who brought it in, Trish was. She had to leave because one of her kids got sick, but she wanted to make sure Ham got it."

"This shit is loud," I said, stuffing it into my boxers.

"The smell of sex should cover it up."

"Huh?"

"I know you fucked Carmen, I can smell it on you from here." To deny the obvious was pointless, so I just waited to see where she was going with this.

"You're not denying it," she said.

"Did you miss the part where I said she's my wife?"

"I heard you loud and clear. Just make sure your dick is clean when I call you back down here."

86

"Iesha, listen…"

"You should go. I've got work to do," she said, moving past me and opening the door.

I stood there stuck for a second, amazed at how I'd just been dismissed like that.

Man, this bitch is crazy, I said to myself. I was nervous about going back to my floor, but I couldn't be lingering with this weed on me. When I got to the top of the stairs I could see Burnette who was watching the floor, but no one on the floor could see me yet.

"Burnette…pssst! Are they still I my cell?" I asked.

Once she shook her head no I was on the move with no time for small talk or distractions. Thankfully, Ham was already in the cell trying to put it back together.

"Yo, everything straight?"

"Yeah, we're good," he replied.

"What made them fuck with us today?"

"Timothy was in the chow hall on his bullshit and we had words."

"Come on, bruh. You know how the game goes. You can't win with that nigga, and we got too much going on to be on their radar all the time."

"I know."

"And why you got Ms. Girl bringing this loud ass weed?" I asked, pulling the package out and tossing it to him.

"Because we need that good green, my nigga. Why does it smell like booty-do?"

I couldn't help laughing at the face he was making, knowing he was smelling the different types of pussy and some good sex.

"Fuck all that, just roll one up. Give me a little something to go holla at Gotti with really quick."

I already had a game plan in my mind of how to solve the problem with Capel. Because I was a fan and student of old school remedies, all I needed to do now was see what it would cost.

"What's shaken, bruh?" I asked Gotti, knocking on his door and closing it behind me once he told me to come in.

"G-mackin.' What's good with you?"

"I need a favor, and it's important."

"Pull up a chair and holla at me."

I did just that and ran down what I needed done, without mentioning Iesha. He didn't need to know all that, plus he'd just figure that I felt some type of way about Capel fucking with me and tossing my cell. He didn't ask any questions, but I could see the wheels turning rapidly in his mind.

"How soon?" he asked.

"A.S.A.P."

"You get me the info tonight and it'll be done by tomorrow. I want an ounce of that fine china."

"Done. I'll holla at you as soon as I've got the info," I said, passing him the weed.

"Good lookin,' son."

I went back to my cell where I found Hambone impatiently waiting to light the blunt he'd rolled in my absence. While he took care of that, I got the phone out of stash, sent Iesha a text explaining what I needed done, and put the phone right back. Truthfully speaking we shouldn't have been smoking with Timothy and Capel on the loose, but we had the window open and plenty of good smelling Muslim oils to cover up the aroma.

I wasn't willing to take a chance on having the phone out though. On the inside our days were full of repetition. Once we had the cell put back together it was time to sit back and chill while they did count.

It never seemed strange to me how I could reach the darkest corners of my mind when I was high. It felt like I was unlocking the door to a room full of secrets and devious plans that were just waiting on me. It was a moment like this when I came up with the brilliant idea of how to stay out of prison when shit hit the fan. Despite my current hotel accommodations, it still wasn't time to bring that plan to light, because I only got one shot at it. Before I made a move, I had to be sure that I'd actually be convicted of the bullshit they were coming at me with.

The way witnesses were disappearing, I had a feeling the case could be dropped at the preliminary. I just needed to lay low and ride it out. Once count was clear I grabbed my shower stuff and I was headed for the water, but I was stopped along the way.

"I n-need to talk to you. Leslie said it would be okay," he said softly, looking around and fidgeting.

I looked towards Leslie's door and saw him standing there watching the exchange. I didn't know the little white dude standing in front of me, but I remembered him because he was the one getting raped in the shower. I looked at him and then back at Leslie who was now summoning us to come to his cell.

"Come on," I said leading the way towards Leslie. Once we were all in the cell with the door closed, I looked at Leslie expectantly.

"He needs your help."

"How's that?" I asked.

"Y-you know what happened to me," he said.

I didn't confirm or deny this I simply waited on him to get to his point.

"I know you don't know me. My name is David, and I'm not supposed to be here."

"None of us are," I replied sarcastically.

"My only crime was trying to buy the affections of a woman, but it turns out she was a seventeen-year-old who'd been forced into a life of prostitution. I was charged with statutory rape, but I swear I didn't force her to do anything!"

"Well, I'm not a lawyer so I'm not sure how I can help."

"A sex offender is automatically thought of as someone who's done something to a child. I'm only twenty-three myself and I'm not that type of person," he insisted.

There was truth to what he said about the stigmatism surrounding that type of crime. Most mufuckas didn't ask for your story on time-sheet Tuesday, because it wasn't what you know, it was what you thought you knew. Just based on what I'd heard so far I understood how he ended up bent over with three big niggas tearing his asshole to pieces.

"What is it you need from me?" I asked.

"I need you to make it stop," he pleaded.

"That don't have anything to do with me."

"I know prison has always been a hear no evil, see no evil, speak no evil atmosphere, but he doesn't deserve this, Zay." Leslie said.

Prison was everything that Leslie described, but it was also the land of politics. It wouldn't be politically correct for me to step into the situation that had absolutely nothing to do with me or mine. Which meant for me to get involved it'd have to be worth it.

"Is this you asking me for a favor, Leslie, or him?"

"It's me asking for him," Leslie replied.

"Tell me, David, why should I get involved? How does that benefit me?"

"W-what do you want?"

"Relax, I'm nowhere near gay so anything sexual is off the table. As for what I want, I want you to explain to me why you're of value."

"My family has money. My mom works for the government, but my dad comes from old money."

"What exactly does your mom do for the government?" I asked.

"Nothing major. She just does transportation and relocation stuff."

I heard the bell ding in my brain like the first round of an old Tyson fight. This kid might be of use after all.

"The guys I saw you with, they don't live on this floor, do they?" I asked.

"No, on the third floor."

"Okay, I'll handle it, but you owe me. And when I call on the favor there better not be any hesitation."

"There won't be, I swear!"

"Leslie, get him moved in here with you and keep him out of the way."

"I can do that," Leslie replied.

"I'll come holla at you both," I said.

I went to the shower wondering if this was just dumb luck for shit to fall in my lap like this. On the other hand, it was kinda in my own best interest to solve the problem before David brought unwanted heat and attention to our floor by hollering rape. When you were doing dirt, you had to keep your surroundings as clean as possible, which meant keeping the bullshit to a minimum. On the other hand, dude's mom could turn into the one piece of the puzzle I was missing.

The one question I needed answered was who the fuck the confidential informant was against me, because they were obviously building their case around that. Kill the head and the body will fall. I got out of the shower with a renewed confidence that I'd be home soon. I just had to play the hand I was dealt.

"Keep a lookout for me," I told Ham, before I kicked him out so I could get myself together.

I covered the window and pulled the phone back out to see if Iesha had come through. Sure enough, everything I needed was there, along with a surprise in the form of an apology for her catching an attitude with me about Carmen. She even promised to make it up to me later, which put a smile on my face. That smile didn't stay there long once I saw the message from Carmen telling me I needed to call her A.S.A.P, and not from a recorded phone. The message seemed normal enough, but I had a bad feeling just the same. Still, I dialed her number.

"Hey, baby, what's up?" I asked.

"Tell me you're not a complete idiot, Zayvion!"

"Huh? What the fuck are you talking about?"

"What I am talking about is two fucking FBI agents showing up at my goddamn house asking if I was doing your dirty work. Apparently three witnesses have wound up dead and you're to blame!"

"I haven't done shit, I'm in fucking prison!" I yelled back.

"And your black ass is gonna stay there if you don't fix this! Fix it like you promised."

Chapter Ten

My mind was a hundred miles and running in every different direction. Weed didn't help and neither did sleep, because every time I closed my eyes I kept seeing the alphabet chasing me. The FBI, ATF and DEA all equaled up to one thing. L-I-F-E! I wasn't no bitch, and neither was a life sentence. The shit Carmen was thinking added up to witness tampering, murder, conspiracy to commit murder, and whatever else they could think of to make it sound good.

I'm a realist so I know I won't be judged by a jury of my peers, but by mufuckas who'd feel safer with me under the jail! I had no choice except to tell Iesha to call off her dogs. She'd been pissed about that. Apparently, her goon was a young nigga out of Louisville named Shmurda, and to her way of thinking with him being a juvenile it didn't matter if he caught a body. He'd already beat a couple anyway, and he was a hood certified standup guy. From my point of view, his loyalty wasn't in question, I just didn't need the heat his actions were bringing.

Innocent people didn't kill witnesses and it was that exact logic the jury would use before casting a unanimous vote to crucify my black ass. I was a man of my word though, because I had Boo Gotti's people take pictures of the nigga Capel's house, his daughter playing at school, his wife out shopping, and his momma sitting in her living room watching TV. Then I sent those pictures to him with a message that let him know if he kept fucking with Iesha I was gonna reach out and fuck with something he loved. I sent her the same information, and so far, she hadn't heard anything else from him.

Sometimes the threat of violence was enough, especially when you targeted what a man loved most. Dying didn't scare most niggas. I mean you could only die once. But the infliction of pain, if done the right way, could break the strongest of men, and that's why you always protected that you loved, if you were bout that life. Or if you were smart, you didn't love it at all. Some niggas played by rules, and that was cute, but the reality was times were changing every day and that meant the rules changed. I didn't have time to keep up, not if I wanted to survive, so I lived by my own rules.

I tried to use logic and reasoning whenever possible, but sometimes you had to say fuck it. Case in point, it was time for me to go have a chat with the ringleader of the dudes who'd turned David's asshole into a wind tunnel. There were a few ways to approach this situation, and I was going with the reasonable one of direct conversation first.

"Big T, what's shakin'?"

"Do I know you?" he asked, glancing up from his chess game.

"Yes and no. Your cousin Peewee is my homeboy and I look out for him from time to time."

"Oh, okay. What's up?"

"I need to holla at you about some important business." He gave the dude he was playing chess with a nod to leave us, and he gave me his undivided attention.

"Listen, I need you to spare little buddy down on my floor, and before you say it, I know it ain't my business," I said.

"Then why you stickin' your nose into it?"

"Because eventually it's gonna cause problems that affect my business. The last thing either of us need is some little white boy hollering rape."

"I don't know about you, but I got forever in this mufucka, so a rape charge doesn't mean shit," he replied seriously.

"I hear you, but it still ain't a good look for me. I like money, my nigga, and unwanted attention doesn't create more money. I'm just asking you to respect the hustle."

"What you eat don't make me shit, so what's in it for me?" he asked.

Part of me felt some type of way that he would ask me some shit like that, but nothing in this world came free. I made sure to check my surroundings before taking the gram of heroin out of my pocket and passing it under the table to him.

"A token of my appreciation," I said. He studied it briefly before putting it in his pocket.

"And how often should I expect these tokens of appreciation?"

I smiled at that question, but I was already thinking about what my next move would be. Kindness should never be taken for weakness, but it was obvious no one ever told this nigga that. He was old school penitentiary, which was a nice way of saying he was a bully that was more prone to using brute force over intelligence. Me, on the other hand, I considered life to be very much like the game sitting on the table between us, and the only way to win was by anticipating your opponent's moves.

"That's a one-time donation, my nigga. Just a show of thanks for understanding that business trumps everything."

"If you wanna buy him it's gonna cost more than that," he replied smiling.

"Tell you what, I'll hit you off with some more this weekend, cool?"

"Yeah, that's cool, but tell him I'll be down tonight for one more ride."

For a moment, I felt myself wanting to smack the grin off his face, but that would be stupid and impulsive on my part.

"I got you," I said, getting up and heading for the stairway that would take me back to my floor.

"What's up, Zay?" CJ called from the doorway.

CJ was a cool ass white boy that I knew from my time in county. He was crazy, but that didn't stop me from taking a liking to him and making sure he ate while we were in the jail together. I knew what it was like to be hungry.

"Just handling some business, CJ, you know how that goes."

"Yeah, I got you."

"I'll get with you later," I said, going downstairs and straight to Leslie's door.

"It's taken care of," I said.

David was sitting on the top bunk watching TV and I could see the weight visibly lift off of him when I said it was over.

"Thank you," he whispered.

"Just remember our arrangement."

"I will, I promise."

"Thanks, Zay." Leslie said.

"I know you wouldn't have asked unless it was important, besides it might turn out to help me more than it did him. Listen, get everything you need to go on lockdown for a couple of days."

"Lockdown? Zay, what…"

"Leslie, don't start asking me questions like you're an inmate when you know damn well you're a convict," I said, stopping whatever ridiculous shit that was coming out of his mouth. Reaching in my pocket I gave him a half of a gram before I headed to Fred's cell.

"What up, my nigga?"

"Chillin,' chillin.' What's up with you?" he asked, motioning for me to come in.

"Just wanted to holla at you really quick. We gonna be locked down within the next couple of hours, so I wanted to make sure you didn't need anything."

"Locked down? Damn. How long?"

"Couple days at the most."

"I'm good on food and shit, what about you?"

"You know it's like Walmart in my house," I replied laughing.

"You got some green?"

"A little something, but that shit is loud, bruh. The oil might not cover it good enough, so you need to have some muscle rub on deck to burn."

"I got that."

"A'ight give me a few minutes," I said, leaving his cell and going to holla at the few select people I dealt with to put them up on game.

Nobody asked how I knew what I knew or what was going on, not because they weren't curious, but because this was the land of don't ask, don't tell. Everybody just went about the business of preparing themselves so they could do their time comfortably. I'd just got out of the shower an hour later when Ms. G came on the floor and announced an emergency lockdown. Of course niggas started moaning and complaining because none of us liked being trapped behind that door for twenty-four hours a day, but everybody moved as instructed. When Ms. G got to Boo Gotti's door I caught the smile she gave him when he winked at her, and then I heard him ask what was going on. Apparently, someone had been stabbed in the shower up on the third floor and it didn't look like he was gonna make it.

That wasn't uncommon. I mean prison is more or less a university for bad guys. What do they really expect to happen when you put all the bad people in one spot, especially when you have those few who feel like they run shit? The only thing that runs prison is the same thing that runs the world, money. You could buy someone's life just as quick as you could another's death, especially since nothing is more dangerous than a man who has nothing to lose. Few people understood why money was the root of all evil. They just saw it as a necessary evil and most days I agreed. I had just enough time to do my hygiene before the door was unlocked and Hambone came in.

"I thought your ass was up here getting into shit," he said.

"You know better than that negro. I'm chillin.'"

"Yeah, whatever, I know you better than that."

"If you say so. Did you pick up from Trish today?"

"Come on, cuzzo, I'm handling mine," he replied, pulling out a Ziploc bag containing powder and pills.

"Boy or girl?" I asked.

"That girl, Ms. China, and them Flintstone pills known as Ecstasy."

"You got orders for X?"

"Yep."

"Listen, don't start getting reckless, my nigga. We on some stick and move type shit, you got me?"

"Yeah, yeah. Relax, you know I ain't no dummy," he said.

It was on the tip of my tongue to say some smart shit, but he'd been selling drugs long enough to know what he was doing. As long as I could keep a low profile and make money, I was good. We spent the next day and a half playing dominoes, high as a mufucka, waiting on shit to blow over. With the compound being on lockdown I couldn't go to medical, but Iesha and Trish took turns coming to see us.

I didn't dare try to move anything though. That would've been some hot shit. On the second day, I thought we were coming off lock when I heard the key turning in my door that morning, but instead it was the shift captain. Captain Fuller was your average looking white guy, but he stayed military pressed with an unreadable look on his face. The only time we'd had any interaction was when I'd had words with a sergeant. Captain Fuller had told me straight up that he'd never side with me or any other inmate over his officer.

Even if I was right I was wrong. I could respect the honesty, but I still went out of my way to stay out of his way. Seeing him at my door at seven a.m. filled me with unease.

"Miller?"

"Yeah, Captain?"

"Get dressed and come with me," he ordered.

Outwardly, I wasn't panicked, but inside I was screaming what the fuck! I knew what this could be about and I prayed I was wrong, but either way I knew I had to keep my mouth shut and my poker face on. I pulled on my jumpsuit and shoes, looking at him until I was sure he got the message not to panic and start flushing shit. If they were coming to tear the cell up they'd be doing it already, and it would be a lot more than just the Captain. Once I was dressed and out the cell he locked the door back and told me to follow him. I felt like asking where we were going could show weakness or fear, like I was worried about something and that would draw suspicion.

One thing I knew for certain was that our destination wouldn't be a secret for too long. When we got downstairs, he stopped in front of the legal visitation room and told me to wait inside. My nerves loosened a little because it was most likely my lawyer with an update on my case. Hopefully, it was good news because I'd had enough drama and bullshit to last me through New Year's.

"Stand up, Miller," a CO ordered, stepping in the room carrying a waist chain, a pair of handcuffs and a black box that fit around the cuffs to restrict movement.

I wasn't nervous now. I was two steps away from full panic! The only time this assortment of gear came out was when an inmate was travelling or being restrained. Neither of these options was good for me.

"What's all the jewelry for?" I asked, trying to be nonchalant.

"You've got an attorney visit."

"Okay. Last time I checked I wasn't a threat to my own defense team, so why the restraints?"

"Your lawyer will explain when he gets here."

I stood up, seeing it was obviously useless to keep asking questions, because this mufucka either didn't have, or wouldn't reveal, the answers. The situation was bad because if a lawyer asked for all of this shit then whatever news he was coming with didn't work in my favor. Once he had me hooked up like jumper cables I was instructed to sit back down and wait. The oldest game in prison was hurry up and wait, and the COs loved to play it, because they knew a nigga ain't have nowhere to go. Petty mufuckas!

"I'm sorry I'm late, Zayvion."

"Late? It's seven-thirty in the damn morning, what time did you plan on getting here, and why am I wearing all this?" I asked, rattling the waist chain for emphasis.

"Okay, first of all you know as your attorney that any conversation we have is privileged."

"I'm aware."

"However, I still don't want you to tell me anything incriminating, because I just don't wanna know."

"Dually noted," I replied, wondering where this was going.

"Okay, so we've got a problem. Apparently, three people who were set to testify against you have turned up dead."

"I didn't…"

"Ah! That's not the issue at hand. The government doesn't believe in coincidences, and the FBI believes you ordered the hits. Fortunately, they can't prove a damn thing. Unfortunately, they convinced the judge to move your preliminary court date up, and subsequently your trial date."

"Move it up? Move it up to when?"

"We're due in court in two hours."

"Two hours?! That can't be legal!"

"Legal? Have you forgotten where you are? If you have, then allow me to be the first to greet you. Welcome to Virginia."

Aryanna

Chapter Eleven

Richmond was the capital of Virginia, and once upon a time it had been as known for its murder rate as D.C. and New Orleans. More murders meant more laws, stricter laws, and a lot less tolerance for the bullshit. Now all this meant that the fear I felt working its way through my bloodstream as we got closer to the federal courthouse was understandable. Rule number one was never let them see you sweat, but right now they had a mufucka feeling like the D.C. sniper on my way to trial.

My mind had a song by the Clipse on repeat running around and around. The title of the track was Virginia and the part that stuck in my head was.

'Ironic, the same place I'm making figures at, that there is the same land they use to hang niggas at. I'm from Virginia.'

The truth in those chords seemed to get louder the closer we got to our destination, but they weren't the least bit comforting. The state slogan was that Virginia was for lovers, but anyone who's been here knew the real slogan was, come on vacation, leave on probation, after a period of incarceration. What the fuck had I gotten myself into?

The only thing I knew for sure was that I couldn't run away from this kind of trouble. I was gonna have to run through it.

"A'ight, Miller, you know how this goes. You're to do what we say when we say, and if you don't you can look forward to us fucking you up on the spot. Any questions?"

I didn't know this CO, but I definitely didn't like his pimple-faced ass. The young boys that worked corrections killed me, because they thought that badge gave them some superiority. They didn't understand that the moment a mufucka got tired of their shit we could permanently turn their satellite off. And it was always the nerd, the chump, or the weird guy from high school that took these jobs and started ego trippin.' I just shook my head at his slick ass comments, but I filed them to the back of my mind, because forgetting has always been something I was bad at.

I was escorted from the car into the back of the courthouse and taken straight to the elevator that took us up one floor. When the elevator door opened, there were men in suits everywhere, and a few women, but they were all the same. Feds. I was led into a courtroom much smaller than what I'd expected. It was intimate in size. There was a crowd of about twenty to thirty people spread out throughout the gallery, but my eyes immediately landed on the woman sitting in the front row behind the table I was being led to.

"Carmen? Baby, how did you know to be here?" I asked, feeling some semblance of calm because she was by my side.

"Your lawyer called me. Come on, babe, you know I got your back no matter what. Right or wrong, I'm always gonna be here."

"I love you for that, babe."

"I love you too, and we're gonna get through this."

I wanted to wrap my arms around her, but the look I was getting from my escorts told me that I'd have to fight them first. I caught sight of my lawyer making his way to my table and I took confidence in the fact that he didn't look nervous. Then again, he got paid way too much not to have an outstanding poker face.

"Alright, Zayvion, here's what's gonna happen. Basically, the prosecution is gonna argue that they have enough to bind this over for trial, and I'm gonna argue that they don't."

"That simple, huh?"

"Yep. The problem is it only takes two or more people to say you're supplying them with drugs in order to make a conspiracy case, and as you know they have eight people saying that."

"So, what's the play?" I asked.

"The play is to try and get all testimony ruled inadmissible as hearsay, because they don't have you on audio or video."

"Will it work?"

"That all depends on if they have dates, times and locations of transactions."

"That's impossible, because I wasn't the one…"

"Ah! I told you I didn't wanna know anything about anything. At least not until we have to go to trial, because then I'll need all the dirt you have."

"If this thing does go to trial, and I'm found guilty, how bad does it look for me?"

"Trust me when I tell you we don't even wanna entertain those thoughts."

"What do you think their plea deal is gonna be?"

"They already sent one and I shot it down."

"Hold up, why would you do that without talking to me?" I asked angrily.

"Because it was ridiculous and I knew you wouldn't like it."

"What was it?"

The whole time we'd been talking he'd been taking papers out of his folder and setting up his workstation, but when I asked that question he kinda froze up. The hesitation was real, which could only mean the numbers were bad.

"Trust me, you don't want it," he replied.

"What was it?"

"All rise," the Bailiff ordered.

"Charles?" I whispered.

"Fifty years, day for day."

Outside of having an orgasm I'd never had my vision instantly fill up with stars until this moment. I tried to process what he'd said, but my brain kept locking on that big ass number he'd spit out. I heard the Bailiff introduce the judge to the court and then I slumped back into my seat, thankful no walking was required at this moment. The prosecution started by first trying to say I was having witnesses killed, but before they could get it out of their mouth good, my lawyer was objecting.

They went to their sworn affidavits next which alleged I was something like Tony Montana, but again my lawyer was on their ass asking for specifics, photos, or any video that could confirm these allegations. Of course, our questions led them right into the heart of their case, which was their confidential informant. According to them their CI could testify to more than a dozen hand-to-hand transactions of both narcotics and guns, as well as lay out my whole operation.

My lawyer tried to find out the identity of this CI, but given the fact that they thought I was knocking witnesses off that didn't fly very far. The prosecution promised to reveal all on the first day of trial, assuring the judge that the CI could be first to testify. They also asked for protection for the remaining witnesses listed in the indictment. I wasn't a lawyer, but none of this shit sounded good to me. If they actually had all these mufuckas testifying against me, plus everything they'd confiscated during their raids, then that was fair ballgame.

I felt like my lawyer could discredit the remaining witnesses, but whoever this CI was could bury me if they knew all that about me. It had to be either one of the people we were supplying with major weight or somebody deep inside my inner circle. I was gonna have to get with Rocko so he could figure this shit out and put a stop to it quick! When my lawyer got to talk, he painted me as something like a model citizen who'd only had an indiscretion in my youth.

A loving father and devoted husband, I mean dude damn near had me believing I was a white guy named Bob from Suburbia! In the end, it wasn't enough though, because my black ass was bound over for trial anyway. After the gavel banged. I was given a few minutes to pow wow with my wife and lawyer.

"So now what?" I asked.

"Now we get ready for real. A motion for discovery will tell me exactly what they have, except for the identity of the CI"

"Well, I can..."

"Ah! I don't wanna know, remember?"

"You did a good job, Mr. Swedish, but tell me, can you get Zay out of this?" Carmen asked.

"I'm gonna do my best, Mrs. Miller. I'm not gonna lie to you, whoever that CI is seems to be their smoking gun. If I can discredit whoever that is the rest will be a walk in the park. Now the first thing I'm gonna need is a list of your movements for the day of the busts."

"A list of her movements, why?" I asked.

"Because I know where you were, and if I can prove where she was that goes towards establishing that you couldn't have had your hands in this deal. It's kinda hard to try you for past deals without evidence of that crime, so if they can't tie you to this one then they can't label you a dealer of drugs and guns."

"You're definitely worth the money I pay you," I said, smiling for the first time.

"Indeed I am, and it's about to cost you fifty-thousand dollars more, but we'll get to that. While your wife and I are locking down her timeline, I'll also be pulling all your phone conversations and the visitation log for about a month before all this. Will I find any surprises?"

"No, I don't talk reckless on the phone, and the only people who came to visit me are my wife, daughter and brother-in-law."

"Brother-in-law?"

"Yeah, Carmen's big brother."

"And where is he?" he asked her.

"Out of town right now," she replied, evasively.

"Okay, that's not important right now. Your trial is three weeks from now, which is a very quick turnaround. I'ma get to work A.S.A.P, but I need the fifty-thousand-dollars before trial starts."

"I'll wire it to you today," Carmen said.

"Okay. In the meantime, I need you to chill, Zayvion. I need everyone around you to chill, understand?"

"I got you," I replied.

"I'll be to visit you in a week or so."

"A'ight thanks, Charles."

"No problem," he said, packing up his briefcase and heading for the door. I thought I'd get a few minutes with Carmen, but the COs were already pulling on me.

"I'll call you when we come off lockdown," I said, winking at her.

She nodded her head and mouthed I love you before I was pushed out the doors and back into the elevator. I knew it wasn't going to be easy, but my lawyer sounded like he had a handle on the situation. I just had to do my part, and right about now I figured that involved me calling in a newly acquired favor. I knew my lawyer didn't want any more witnesses having a dirt party, but it was still important to know who the CI was so we could prepare for my case.

My three-week trial wait would be here before I knew it, so we had to get to work A.S.A.P. I spent the ride back to prison going over all the possible suspects I could come up with for who might be telling on me, but in truth, the list was too long. Not because I dealt with a lot of mufuckas, but because of the hatred that came with success. Niggas were mad instead of motivated to go get their own, wasting their days wishing for an empire instead of building one brick by brick.

Was I supposed to be sorry and apologize for making it do what it does? The truth was that drugs sold themselves, so if a nigga couldn't do something as simple as envisioning having the finer things in life then that was his problem. I'd never shed a tear for paying the price of admissions when it came to the game, and I wasn't gonna let some fuck nigga bring me down either. We got back to the prison at what would've been lunchtime, and I was given a bag with a couple of bologna sandwiches to eat in the legal visit room once my travel gear was removed.

It had been almost two whole days of lockdown, which meant we were due to be let out anytime as long as no one opened their mouth. Admittedly, that was a rare occurrence in prison. I never understood why mufuckas snitched in here like they were going home off the info they were gagging to give up. It really fucked me up to see a nigga who took his case to trial, and stood ten toes tall, turn into someone who pointed a finger in order to maintain the creature comforts of prison. I guess gas station food and being able to watch TV meant a lot to certain people though. It was just as crazy to see a mufucka with a life sentence, an elbow, who wouldn't fight. Let alone kill a nigga. Wasn't no coming back from a life sentence in Virginia. That was a guaranteed six-hundred-year pill to swallow.

So how could a nigga with forever allow himself to be called everything but a child of god, have his shit taken, or be disrespected in the slightest? I don't know, but I'd damn sure seen it. Sometimes up was down, and a rose grew from concrete with no thorns.

"You finished eating, Miller?" Captain Fuller asked.

"Yeah, I'm done."

"Follow me then."

I threw my trash away and followed him up the stairs, wondering if I should send a note to David's cell or wait until we come off of lock. Time was of the essence when it came to building my defense, but I doubted Leslie had a cell phone over there anyway for him to make the necessary call.

"When do we come off lock, Captain?" I asked.

He ignored me completely, acknowledging my presence when he stopped in front of medical to wait on me to catch up.

"I got some bad news, Miller."

"What's that?"

"I've been instructed to put you in the hole under investigation."

"What? Why?"

"Because you know what happened upstairs."

Chapter Twelve

One of the things I hated more than anything about prison was their kangaroo court system. I could understand the idea of consequences for your actions when you fucked up, but the way they would throw a nigga in the dungeon without proof of any wrong doing was an abuse of power. They called it an investigation, but what they really meant is we think you did something, we can't prove you did, so we're gonna make you sweat.

Now for the weak niggas who couldn't bid without their creature comforts, this was when they started singing like Whitney Houston in the eighties and nineties, before crack became whack. I was a different caliber dude though, so a little time in the box wouldn't make or break me, it was just a vacation. The good news was that I was put in the cells that were right across from the main hole, which was undergoing massive renovation and construction. The bad news was that the cockroaches were as big as dogs, the water tasted like it was purified in Mexico, and it was hot enough for the devil to need sunblock in this bitch.

I spent my first night standing at the door, dripping wet, listening to niggas scream until the sun came up. I'd been to the hole before, but every hole was different in its own way. In county, we had to sleep on concrete slabs for sixteen out of twenty-four hours, in temperatures that would've had Santa clause looking for warmer weather or a job change. The food was nothing more than a mess of bread, old vegetables and raisins all combined together. Still, that type of hell didn't prepare me for this one. I'd spent the better part of day two laying on a mat that stuck to me better than a bottle of Elmer's, hoping the roaches didn't wanna fight, because I was out numbered. I thought I was going mad because it sounded like someone was calling my name, and then the front door opened.

"Miller!"

"B-back here," I replied, voice cracking from lack of usage. The roaches were good company, but they didn't talk much.

"I'm here to check your vitals," she said, stopping in front of the door.

I got up and went to the bars, finding a nurse I'd never seen before standing there. I didn't know where she'd been hiding, but she was beautiful. Standing five feet seven inches with shoulder length dirty blonde hair and an athletic build, I admired everything about her.

"Wow," I uttered, further transfixed by her stunning smile.

"Would you mind sticking your arm through the slot so I can put the blood pressure cuff on you?"

I did as requested, loving how soft her hands felt against my skin, but stopping myself when my mind wandered towards how soft they'd feel on other places.

"What's your name?" I asked.

"Alexis."

"Did you just start here?"

"No, I've been here for a while, but I usually only work the hole."

"Ah, that's why I haven't seen you."

"That doesn't mean I don't know who you are," she replied, smiling again.

"Really?"

"Mmhmm. Iesha told me to come check on you," she whispered, passing me a note.

"Thanks."

"You're welcome. She wanted me to bring something else, but I can't lose my job. I'm a single mom."

"I can respect that and I understand. How many kids do you have?"

"Three."

"Shut up."

"What?" she asked.

"I just mean you look good to be a mother of three."

The sight of her blushing made her even more beautiful, but I knew to keep my conversation light. No need to have Iesha go off the deep end.

"Thank you," she said, taking the blood pressure cuff off and grabbing the thermometer to take my temperature.

I had to suppress my baser instincts, because I wanted to grab her hand and suck on her delicate fingers until her panties were soaked. The eye contact she was giving me was amazing, and I swear we were speaking with our own language.

"So do you like working in the hole?" I asked, once she'd removed the thermometer.

"Some days. Some days the guys are just too damn disrespectful to tolerate, but I've got thick skin for a little white girl."

"You've got a little country in you too," I commented, noticing the twang in her voice.

"Is there something wrong with that?"

"Not at all, a southern belle is timeless and sexy."

"Is that right?" she asked smiling.

"That's just my personal opinion."

"I'll remember that. You seem to be doing okay health wise back here, Mr. Miller. Do you know how long you'll be back here?"

"I don't, and please call me Zay."

"Uh...I don't think Iesha would like that," she whispered.

"Probably not, but do it anyway."

Her laughter was sweet, like listening to an old R. Kelly song. I wanted to really kick it with her, but I could see the CO lurking just out of my vision.

"Is there anything you need?" she asked.

"The food sucks and some home cooking would be nice."

"I'm not even going to tell you what I brought for lunch then."

"What?"

"You don't wanna know," she said, packing all her medical supplies back into her bag.

"It's okay, tell me."

"Smothered pork chops, rice, greens and a little banana pudding."

"Damn! You gonna eat all that?"

"Hell yeah!" she replied, laughing again.

"Did you cook it?"

"I sure did. My accent ain't the only thing from the south."

"I heard that. Well you enjoy that meal for the both of us."

"I can do that. Hopefully you'll be out of here soon, but I'll check on you tomorrow."

I wanted to ask her to stay, but I knew that couldn't realistically happen. I did watch her walk away though, admiring every swing of her hips and the nice ass she had. I couldn't deny that I had fantasies of knocking the doors off the white girl from the south. Part of the attraction was the country twang, but the other part was knowing that the moment I slung dick to her all her racists ancestors would turn over in their graves.

I could hear them now screaming in protest as she screamed in ecstasy, and of course, she'd use all the back channels she knew to find out why I was in here, and all she'd come up with is that I was seen on the third floor on camera a couple hours before the stabbing. The nigga who got stabbed was Big T, the same one I'd been seen talking to, so they were basically holding me hostage until they determined what I knew. How they were gonna tell me what I knew was beyond my comprehension because they weren't mind readers!

Big T was only a knock away from death's door, they couldn't pinpoint who did it, so all I had to do was ride it out, because they only had a week to conclude their investigation. The problem was I didn't have a week to waste when I needed to be preparing for the fight of my life. Her letter did come with some good news though, because she said she'd been to the doctor and our baby was healthy and growing nicely. Next time she went we'd be able to tell the sex if we wanted to know.

I definitely wanted to know, but my feelings were conflicted. I knew if it was a boy she'd insist we name him Zayvion Jr., but what happened if I got Carmen pregnant with a little man too? It seemed like there was a potential for catastrophe at every turn! I had enough on my mind without adding this to it, so I chose to try and sleep in hopes that my subconscious could work some shit out. It was wishful thinking though because as soon as I turned the lights out my mind went straight to the current mystery it wanted to solve.

Alexis. The way her name rolled off my tongue made me wonder how she would taste on this same tongue. It was thoughts like these that carried me off to sleep, and even though I didn't dream of her, I woke up to a surprise. Just inside my door, out of sight of anyone but me locked in my cell, was a Tupperware container. I opened it to find a smothered pork chop, rice and greens. On the floor, next to it was a note that said she'd ate the banana pudding with a smiley face in place of a signature. I couldn't help smiling as I ate the best breakfast I could remember having in a long time.

The food was so good that it made the monotony of another day in here pass with ease, and I was actually able to formulate a plan. I had to hope Alexis would return as promised, because I needed to get a message out, but I hadn't been given any of my property so I didn't have the pen, paper, stamps or envelope required. Plus, snail mail took too damn long. I'd almost given up hope when I heard the front door open, and then there she was standing in front of my cell.

"How you holding up, Mr. Miller?"

"I'm good, nurse, how about you?"

"I'm doing fine," she replied, motioning for me to stick my arm through the bars to have my blood pressure checked. I held up her container and after she gave me the all clear sign I passed it to her.

"Amazing," I said.

"Thank you."

"Listen, I need you to relay a message," I whispered. She nodded and kept her hands busy with her work.

"Tell Iesha to call Carmen and let her know what's going on."

"Is that it?"

"Yeah, it'll be handled from there."

"Okay, I got you," she replied.

"Really?"

"Yeah...why are you looking at me like that?"

"It's funny, because that's something I always say. I got you."

"Oh. So, did they tell you when you're getting out of here?"

"Nah, but once that call is made I'll know something. You're gonna miss me when I'm gone, huh?"

"I don't even know you," she replied laughing.

"Do you want to?" I asked, just loud enough for her to hear. She shrugged her shoulders. But the smile never left her face.

"You know where to find me," I told her.

"You have a good night, Zayvion."

"And you too, Alexis."

The look in her eyes seemed to be somewhat challenging, but I found the heat that came with it more interesting. She put her stuff back into her bag and started to leave, but I got one final look when she turned at the door and smiled again. Damn, her smile was gorgeous! The memory of it kept me company through the night and midway through my fourth day, until my door was opened and I was pronounced free to return to general population. I knew I owed this turn of events to my wife, because she probably called up here and went ape shit on the administration.

I've been on the receiving end of that attitude. It would make the pope question God. When I emerged from the dungeon I was glad to see other inmates in the hall, which meant the lockdown was over. As soon as I made it through the gates back on my floor I had mufuckas coming from everywhere trying to holla at me and find out what happened, but my focus was on a shower. That hot water was calling me!

"My nigga!" Hambone said, when I came through the door.

"What up, fam? Everything straight?"

"Yeah, but I had to get rid of the dope before it fell."

"Where's the money?"

"I already sent it to Carmen, you know I don't play no games."

"Good looking. When did you come off of lockdown?"

"Yesterday. Word is dude died, but they knew he was a booty bandit so they chalked it up to some shit going wrong."

"Sounds about right. I'm bout to hit the shower really quick," I said, getting my stuff together.

"I'll have a blunt for you when you come out."

Once I had everything I needed I was on my way to the rain box, but I had to make a detour first.

"Welcome back," Leslie said, opening the door for me to come in his cell. I found David sitting in the same place he was the last time I saw him.

"It's time. I need to call in that favor from you."

Chapter Thirteen

The race was on. I could feel the clock winding down as my trial date drew closer, and I was starting to feel the pressure now that I was out of the hole and moving around. When I'd gotten out of the shower, I made putting David on the phone with his mom my first order of business. The conversation was definitely awkward because he wouldn't give her details about what happened, only that I'd saved his life and made things bearable. When it was my turn to speak to her I kinda had to dance around the fact that I was fighting a case now and make it seem like something that already happened.

Once she started digging she'd know the truth, but David wouldn't, which meant that was one less person I had to worry about. With everything going on I felt like I had to close ranks like my mom had taught me. That meant no new friends, and if I didn't fuck with you, then I didn't fuck with you, it was that simple. I tried to call Rocko so we could put our heads together about who could possibly be pointing the finger at me, but he was making a run so we had to postpone that until later. When you were riding around with work in your car your attention damn well better be on the task at hand, because once them blue lights got behind you the game was over.

After handling as much business as possible I kicked back and talked to Carmen and Ariel, needing to bond with them because it seemed like forever since we'd done that. Of course, in the middle of it my baby girl asked the question that broke a nigga every time he heard it, "Daddy when are you coming home?" I was fortunate to have a daughter young enough to forget that I was absent, provided that I went home at the end of trial. But I knew a lot of dudes that got asked this question by kids just old enough to remember dad missing the first day of

119

kindergarten, and their answer was the same as mine. Soon, daddy will be home soon. I hated lying to my daughter, but she didn't need to carry the weight of uncertainty like I was. She deserved to be a child, innocent and loved and as her father it was my job to make sure she stayed that way as long as possible.

I told Carmen to make sure they made it up here for visitation, and that we were gonna have to give Ariel both days this week. It went without saying that our daughter's needs came before ours, but the fact that Carmen didn't so much as take a deep breath made me appreciate my decision to have a baby with her. I was still huddled up on the phone with her when a knock at the door proceeded the ambush of my niggas telling me I had to come on out the cell and kick it. After making my apologies, I told Carmen I'd call her later and stepped out the cell to find a big ass spread on the table. It was cakes, cookies and honeybuns everywhere, plus somebody had made a pizza and some nachos.

"Damn, who put it down like this?" I asked.

"Come on, son, you know when a nigga is fresh out the hooskow a meal gotta go down," Boo Gotti said, passing me a soda.

"Who cooked?" I asked looking around the table.

"I did," Leslie called from his door.

"Good! That means I ain't gotta worry about dying, because you niggas cooking skills is suspect," I said laughing.

It was me, Gotti, Ham, Double Oh, and Fred at the table, talkin' shit and eating like it was Thanksgiving. Everybody didn't fuck with Leslie the way I did, but it was understandable and his feelings weren't hurt by people's shade. Still I had to make sure he had a plate. People who'd never been on the inside might find it weird how we operated, but in here we learned to be each other's family. When I needed advice, I knew

I could go to the old heads and they'd dispense it like a wise uncle. Nine times out of ten they'd be the one to pull you to the side and kick you in your ass for fucking up too.

When there was a situation, I could go to my closest niggas who were like brothers and they would back whatever my play was. Society viewed us as animals, but really, we were just the black sheep of America's families. Days like today made that even more apparent to me, because these niggas breaking bread with me, these hardened killers, dope dealers, and gangbangers have enough consideration for their fellow man to do something that would make me feel normal again. That's what I called real nigga shit. We sat around and ate until our stomachs started to hurt, and then someone started talking shit, which brought the cards out. It wasn't spades though. We decided to play dirty hearts for cups of hot shower water as the penalty.

"Somebody ass gonna throw up tonight," I declared, slamming the queen of spade on the table so everybody knew I was sportin' that bitch.

I had a side bet with Ham that it was gonna be Fred who upchucked first, because he was already trying to switch from water to push-ups after the first game. He managed to avoid the target I put on his back for the first hour, but by the time they called pill call I had him on his knees hugging his toilet. We all were in tears watching him heave from his spine and try to cuss us out at the same time, and it was definitely a moment not to be forgotten soon. I wanted to stay and try to send Boo Gotti with him, but I wanted to see Iesha even more. It seemed like forever since we'd been together and I knew she was needing this dick as much as I needed to give it to her.

"What up, Davis?"

"Oh I see they let you out of purgatory?"

"They did. You know they were on their bullshit anyway."

"I hear you. Go ahead and get your breathing treatment, the nurse is waiting on you."

"Cool," I replied making my way into medical. I expected to see Iesha sitting behind the desk, but no one was there. I was halfway down the hallway when I heard her voice.

"Can I help you, Mr. Miller?"

"I thought I told you to call me Zay."

"I prefer your full name, Zayvion," Alexis replied, smiling.

"What are you doing here, and where's Iesha?"

"Come on," she said, motioning me to follow her into the exam room.

"Is everything okay?" I asked once the door was closed.

"As far as I know everything is fine, she just called in sick, so I'm filling in."

"Okay, I'll call her."

"Do you need your breathing treatment?" she asked, causing me to pause with my hand on the doorknob.

"Uh, no that's just a code we use to-uh, spend time together."

"Oh. Okay I get it," she replied blushing a deep red.

"Yeah, you could get it," I mumbled.

"What?"

"Nothing, I was talking to myself."

"Well, if you keep that up they might put you back in the room by yourself."

"Would you come to visit me again?"

"Would you want me to?"

"Are you bringing some of that home cooking?" I asked, rubbing my stomach and remembering the taste of that pork chop.

"Ah, so you just want me for my food," she replied laughing. I let go of the doorknob and took a step towards her.

"Maybe I want more than that."

"Oh yeah…like what?"

Another two steps brought me only a whisper from her body, but I didn't touch her. It felt like I was playing with fire in this moment as I stared into her eyes. A lot was at risk if we continued this dance, but I didn't know if it was worth it.

"I need to be honest with you."

"Okay."

"You know my situation with Iesha, but I'm also married too. My wife ain't here, so understandably that's not your problem, but you and Iesha work together."

"Yeah, we do. But I don't owe her nothing."

"So what are you saying?" I asked.

"What are you asking, Zayvion?"

Taking her face in my hands I kissed her softly, enjoying the warmth and taste of her mouth. Her hesitation was brief and then her tongue found mine in a dance of introduction. I could feel the vibration of her heartbeat just in her mouth, and before I knew it I found my hand inside her panties seeking to find another type of rhythmic throbbing.

"Zay…Zay…wait," she paused grabbing ahold of my wrist, but my fingers were already on her clit and I could see the clouds shifting in her beautiful blue eyes.

Our kisses became deeper, more thorough, but I never neglected the massage I was giving her. Finally, I felt pressure lessen on my wrist and I was allowed a peek inside, catching the moan that erupted from somewhere in her throat when I stuck my finger farther in her. She was so tight that I didn't dare try two fingers, but so wet that I wanted to drink from her pussy like it contained all the secrets to life.

"Zay, w-we can't have sex. We can't h-have sex," she murmured.

But her body was speaking a different language. Her body was calling for that dick. I played a song inside her while slowly pulling her panties and pants to the floor, quickly lifting her up and putting her on the exam table without missing a note.

"Oh god, Zayvion!' she panted harder, wrapping her arms around me as her body started to move against my hand.

Pulling her to the edge of the table, I stepped in between her legs with my dick throbbing in my hand. I pulled my finger out and gave her what I knew she craved, pushing inside her an inch at a time so I wouldn't hurt her. Once I was all the way inside I pulled back and delivered a pounding blow that unleashed an orgasm that rocked her body like she was possessed. I dove inside her again and again. Lost in the tropical rains of her delicious juices, but she brought me back to reality quick.

"Stop. Zay, stop," she said.

"What's wrong?" I asked, still buried inside her, but not moving. Her eyes swam with uncertainty and fear.

"We can't do this, I c-can't do this." she replied putting her hands on my chest.

The animal in me wanted to keep fucking her, but the man in me made me back up until the two were no longer one. I watched as she got down off the table and got dressed, noticing the way she avoided eye contact with me.

"Did I do something wrong?" I asked, confused about what had just happened.

"It's not you, I-I'm just like this. I don't even know you and we were about to…"

"I get it, but I thought you liked me."

"I do, Zayvion, and I respect you even more now, because the average guy in your situation wouldn't have stopped when I asked him to."

"Okay, so what's the problem, Alexis? If you like me and I like you then we should see where this goes."

"Where this goes? You mean while you're locked up, because you did say you were married and you have a mistress already."

"You're right," I said fixing my clothes.

"Zayvion, wait," she called, stopping me before I opened the door.

"Listen, I didn't mean that I don't wanna get to know you. It's just, sex is a big deal."

"Are you worried I'll get you pregnant, because I take care of…"

"It's not that, I can't have any more kids. I just wanna be valued more than sex."

"I get that. I apologize for making you think I only wanted some pussy."

"I didn't say that! I just think we should know each other better."

"Like I said before you know where to find me," I said, opening the door and walking out.

I truly did understand what she was saying, but her timing was beyond mind blowing. She was really lucky I was a stand-up nigga, because it took a giant to climb out of some pussy once you were in it. I couldn't stress over this situation though, I already had enough on my plate to last me a lifetime. My sexual frustration was real right now. I had to catch myself, because I was eyeing Davis' big ugly ass as I walked out of medical like I would take her down. I didn't need them types of problems in my life.

Back upstairs I fired up a blunt and texted Iesha to make sure my baby was okay. Our child may not have been planned, but to lose him or her would still devastate me.

"Yo, Zay, let me holla at you really quick," Fred said coming to my door. I waved him in and he grabbed a seat in the chair.

"What up?"

"Is everything gonna be straight this week?"

"Yeah. Business has been running smoothly from the other side and the money is right. Are you getting your gap?"

"Yeah, my fam is looking out for me. I'm just checking, because mufuckas was panicking when you got snatched up."

"We good, bruh."

"You know I'ma be getting classified soon, which means I'll be leaving here. I'm trying to keep eating, so what I gotta do to make sure that happens?"

"All you gotta do is make sure you stay in contact, my nigga. That's my word. I'll handle the rest."

"My nigga," he replied saluting me.

"I got you, ole weak stomach ass!"

"Man, fuck you," he said, laughing as he left the cell.

Iesha still hadn't texted me back, so I decided to call it a night, hoping I'd get some good sleep considering the lack of it the past few days. It definitely felt good to lay down and not have plastic sticking to me. As soon as I closed my eyes the fight was over, but all too soon I was jolted awake by a banging on my door. I didn't know who it was, but I could barely make out the words that my cousin needed me to come to breakfast.

I wanted to cuss out the messenger and the mufucka who sent the message, but I knew Ham wouldn't send for me unless he had a damn good reason. It took me a few minutes to roll out of bed and put a toothbrush in my mouth, but when they announced chow call over the intercom I was ready to roll. As a kid, I'd heard that breakfast was supposed to be the most important meal of the day, but the problem with breakfast in prison was that it happened too damn early.

If the sun wasn't even considering rising yet, what the hell was my black ass doing up? On top of that, to get up for some cold eggs and some oatmeal that was entirely too photo realistic to how vomit looked made no sense. The food wasn't worth the plastic trays it came on, let alone the walk, so Hambone better have some serious money on his mind. Since I didn't know what he wanted I couldn't bring anything with me, but we had runners for emergency situations.

"What you doing up this early?" Leslie asked when I passed him standing in his doorway sipping some coffee.

"I know right. My ignorant ass cousin wants me for something. I'm not staying to eat though, so can you whip something up for breakfast?"

"I'll see what I can do," he replied.

I made my way down the stairs contemplating what I was gonna do with my day. Hopefully, my lawyer paid me a visit so we could talk strategy.

"Ah, what the fuck!"

I screamed feeling a sharp pain in my back as someone pushed me from behind. I managed to brace myself to avoid falling on my face or tumbling down the stairs and breaking my neck. I didn't know what was going on, but staying on the ground could mean death. I tried to get up, but the pain in my back was so lethal that my vision swam and I was forced back to the ground to regroup. Taking a deep breath, I made the agonizing roll from my stomach to my back in hopes of sliding myself to a standing position with the help of the stairs and the railing. The moment I saw blood on the walls all thoughts and plans vanished from my mind. In that moment, I knew the pain I felt didn't come from the fall. It came from being stabbed.

Aryanna

Chapter Fourteen

"Hold on, Zay, we're gonna get you to a hospital."

"W-when?" I grunted in pain. It felt like I'd been laying on this cheap exam room table bleeding out for hours. There was no doubt I left a trail of blood throughout the hall as two niggas had carried me down to medical. All I kept hearing was that an ambulance was on the way.

The pain was so intense that I was drifting in and out of consciousness. I didn't know how long I'd laid in that stairway in a growing pool of my own blood, but it was someone coming up the stairs who discovered me, which meant they'd at least had time to eat. I never saw who actually stabbed me, because they vanished as quickly and as quietly as they came.

I'd never been stabbed before, but it was even more terrifying for it to happen in prison, because medical transportation was not a fast thing.

"The ambulance is almost here, just keep holding on. Do you know who did this to you?" Alexis asked.

"N-no."

And even if I did I couldn't say, but I didn't voice this. I didn't want whoever stabbed me to be caught by the administration, because then he'd be transferred away from here, and we wouldn't be allowed at the same location together. That didn't work for me, there was no way a nigga was literally gonna put a knife in my back and I wasn't gonna get him. I didn't want the COs and their kangaroo court involved. I wanted that dish that was best served cold.

"Alexis!" I screamed when she put more pressure on my wound, damn near causing me to levitate off the table.

"I'm sorry, but I gotta keep the pressure on it to stop the bleeding. It looks like two stab wounds and I think one hit your kidney."

That news wasn't encouraging at all, but I took comfort in the fact she was the one trying to save my life. I really had to respect her professionalism right now, because if it had been Iesha she might've come all the way unglued. It was hard to believe it was actually me laying on the table right now. I didn't fuck with nobody to make them wanna do shit like this, unless they were just jealous because of the moves I was making. Even if that was the case though, a mufucka ain't have to do all this, I would've given him a job or something.

"His ride's here," a CO said opening the door, preceding the stretcher.

"Zay, this is gonna hurt, but we gotta move you," Alexis said taking my hand. All I could do was hold onto her tightly and grit my teeth as they slid me onto the stretcher and strapped me down.

"Alexis, stay," I said, not releasing her hand when she tried to back up.

"I-I can't. I..."

"Please."

I could see the indecision in her eyes. Maybe she was worried about how this all would look, or maybe she didn't wanna see me die on the way to the hospital. For me it was important that she come, because I had no idea who I could trust. And if I was gonna die then I needed to be looking into the eyes of someone without ulterior motives. There was too much pain to articulate all of this in the moment, but I prayed the way I was squeezing her hand and the look in my eyes said what I was unable to.

"We gotta go," I heard someone say from behind me.

I used what strength I had to pull her towards me when the stretcher started moving, and thankfully I didn't meet another resistance on her part. The ride through the halls was fast and loose, but when we got outside it took a bumpy turn that had me gasping in pain and fighting not to have my bowels loosen. The last thing I wanted to do was shit on myself! Finally, they got me into the back of the ambulance, but that didn't stop the black dots I saw swimming in my field of vision. I tried regulating my breathing hoping that would help, but it felt like someone was adjusting the lighting in the room.

"Alexis," I murmured.

"I'm here, I'm not going anywhere."

Those were the last words I heard before the curtains closed for a while. When I stepped back into the light I was zooming down a hospital corridor catching words like 'kidney,' 'blood type,' 'next of kin,' nothing anyone wanted to hear in my current position. I didn't know the full prognosis, the only thing I did know was that I was still holding Alexis' hand and that gave me comfort when someone turned off the lights again. Being unconscious wasn't the dream-like state I'd always heard it to be. It was more like drifting on a piece of plywood through the swamps of Louisiana.

Some might say that didn't sound so bad, but they weren't taking into consideration the predators that lurked in that murky water. The swamp had claimed lives without telling the story, so to me the feeling was like waiting on death to choose you. When I came around again I was hooked up to a bunch of machines in a hospital bed, feeling decent from whatever dope they'd shot me up with. I was in a room by myself, but I was handcuffed to my bed, which probably meant there was a CO somewhere within shouting distance.

Even with the good drugs in my system I was still scared to move, because I didn't want that pain I'd been feeling. One thing I knew for sure was that I'd rather be shot than to ever be stabbed again! The burning sensation that came from a knife was damn near beyond words, but I was glad to have lived through it. I couldn't imagine the pain I would've caused my wife and daughter if I would've died in a dirty prison stairway. And what about my child that had yet to enter this world, how cheated would he or she have felt if I wouldn't have lived to meet them even once?

I could admit to making some less than wise decisions in my life, but with this second chance I knew one thing I was gonna do different for certain. I was gonna live. It didn't matter what it cost me, or how many niggas I had to put in the ground to maintain my right to breathe. When it came down to me or them, I had to choose me every time.

"How are you feeling?" Alexis asked, coming through the hospital room door.

"I'm okay. You're still here."

"I told you I wasn't going anywhere and I try to keep my word."

"I like that," I said, smiling for the first time in a while.

"So, are you gonna tell me what happened?" she asked, pulling up a chair next to my bed.

"I was going to breakfast and I felt a sharp pain in my back right before someone pushed me."

"And you don't know who it was?"

"No."

"Would you tell me if you did?" she asked, fixing me with a stare that said lying to her would be stupid.

"If you asked because you wanted to know, then yes. But if it was for the purposes of notifying the proper people, then no."

"And how would you know my intentions?"

"I'd ask you. So far you seem to be a woman of your word. Let me ask you something though, how bad was it?"

"Well, if the weapon had been longer or a flat blade instead of more of an icepick you would've definitely died. Your body is strong though, and it nicked your kidney versus spearing it. You'll live, and you'll have a few new scars."

"I have you to thank for my life."

"I was just doing my job."

"You may see it that way, but it's deeper than that with me. From this day forward I got you."

"What does that mean?" she asked warily.

"It means that if you need something, I'm the one you need to come see. Your kids are now my kids and if they need something then you come to me."

"I...I can't do that..."

"It's not really something that's open to negotiation. I'm in your debt and I'm gonna pay you back."

"How about you just be a good person and we'll call it even."

"You don't think I'm a good person?" I asked in mock surprise.

"I didn't say that. I'm sure you're someone who does only what they have to do, but it's obvious that whatever you're doing caused this," she replied, gesturing towards me lying in a hospital bed.

"It's all part of the game."

"Is that what you're gonna tell your kids?" she asked, taking my hand in hers.

"Kids?"

"I know you have a little girl and I know Iesha's pregnant."

"Damn, how close are y'all?" I asked, annoyed that my business seemed to be public knowledge.

"Not that close really, but she kinda let it slip when I called her."

"You called her?"

"Yeah, I figured she might want to know what happened to you. Even if it is only sex, I thought she would still care."

"Being with me could never be described as 'only sex.' It's never less than good sex," I said, smiling at the blush that quickly spread across her face.

"Something you like to add to that statement?" I asked.

"Nope, not a damn thing," she replied laughing.

"Listen, all jokes aside. I'm sorry if I hurt you when-uh-you know."

"It didn't hurt."

"Are you sure?" I asked.

"Trust me."

She was still blushing something fierce, but when our eyes met I thought I saw her remembering what had happened between us. I couldn't consider three strokes a mission accomplished, because in truth I wanted to make her climb the walls. The way she climaxed would be pure motivation for me to keep smashing her until I was sure she was mine.

"Can I ask you a question?"

"Sure," she replied.

"When was the last time you actually had sex?"

"Wh-what? You can't ask me that." Her shock at my question made me laugh, which I quickly discovered was a bad idea because I brought intense pain ripping through my body.

"God that hurt," I said breathing heavily.

"Are you okay?" she asked, shooting up out of her chair to hover over me.

"Yeah, but laughing ain't a good idea."

"I'm sorry. Your question caught me off guard."

"Really, why?"

"Because it's…it's personal."

"Really." I said giving her a look meant to convey how far past personal we were. She sat back in her chair and looked at me, but didn't say anything.

"In case it wasn't obvious, I'm pretty good at keeping a secret," I said.

"It's not that, it's just embarrassing."

"I'm not the type to judge. I could tell it's been a while though, I mean you came instantly."

"Are we really having this conversation right now?" she asked, blushing harder.

"Is there another conversation you wanna have? I mean you did say we should get to know each other better."

"I said that?" she asked. I tried to fight the laughter bubbling in my throat, but my eyes said enough because she started laughing.

"You're persistent!"

"I've been told that," I replied.

"Okay, you're right, it's been a while. I've got three kids and two jobs that keep me so busy I'm lucky I know what sleep is."

"Some things can't be neglected, sweetheart."

"I wish it were that simple, Zay, but I don't just sleep with anyone."

"I can respect that. What do you look for in a man?"

"The usual things any woman would want. Someone kind, considerate, understanding, honest. Obviously, someone who's man enough to accept the responsibility of another man's children."

"Could you accept another woman's children?" I asked.

"Of course, but I wouldn't walk into that situation unless I was serious with the guy in a long-term type of way. I'd never play with a child's emotions or give them false hope."

"No, you don't seem like that type. You're a good woman and those are hard to find, but luckily I know what to do with mine."

"Oh yeah, what's that?" she asked with a sly smile.

"I can show…"

"Oh, my God, Zay! Baby, are you alright?" Iesha asked, rushing into the room and to my bedside.

"I'm fine. Thanks to Alexis."

"When she called me I completely lost it! I don't know what I'd do if anything happened to you," she said, taking the hand that Alexis had held a moment ago.

"I'm fine, Iesha, stop worrying."

"Alexis, thank you so much for saving his life and for calling me."

"It's no problem, I was just doing the job. Miller, you hang in there and I'll see you later," Alexis said, backing away towards the door.

"Alexis, wait I…"

"Zayvion! Baby, are you okay? Oh, my God I thought I'd lost you," Carmen cried from the door.

Chapter Fifteen

I'd never had a moment sober me so fast as this one. Hospital drugs are amazing, but there were three women standing in front of me that weren't ever supposed to be in the same room, and my brain immediately cleared. This shit could go bad real fucking quick if I didn't tread lightly.

"I'm fine, babe, the nurses did their job and saved my life."

Carmen's tears were coming so fast that I don't know how she could even see in order to get to my bed, but in seconds she was by my side clinging to me. I held onto her the best I could, given the fact that Iesha hadn't relinquished my hand. Looking at Alexis I sent her a silent plea to get Iesha out of here before shit went wrong.

"Miller, we're gonna go see how long they're admitting you for. Come on, Iesha," Alexis called from the door.

"You go ahead, I'm staying here," she replied with a look of defiance aimed at me. Now was not the time for shit to hit the fan, but in situations like this there never was a good time to be caught up.

"Baby, what happened?" Carmen asked. I ran the story down to her, knowing Iesha was listening too, because it was her first time hearing it.

"You don't know who it was?" Iesha asked.

"Hold up, you can't answer that. She works for the prison," Carmen said.

"I work for Zayvion," Iesha replied matter-of-factly.

When I looked at Carmen I saw her finally analyzing the whole situation, which meant shit was about to go bad.

"If you're gonna take that approach, then let's get it all the way correct, sweetheart. You work for me. I'm the one collecting the money. I'm the head of this household while my man is away, and make no mistake, I'm the one he's coming home to. Now if you don't mind, I'd like a moment alone with my husband."

"You know what…"

"Chill, both of you," I said, fearing that they'd be rolling on the floor in a few minutes.

"Carmen, everyone knows who you are, so there ain't no need to beat on your chest. Now I don't know what impression you've had of Iesha, but if we weren't at least friends do you think she'd be risking her own freedom to bring me shit?"

"She's in it for the money."

"That may be true, but it doesn't negate the fact that we're cool and I almost died today. Stop acting like you don't know what it's like to lose a friend."

"Well, your friend doesn't need to be asking questions that sound like they're coming from her official company."

"Carmen, I asked that question because I'm gonna have the mufucka taken care of. I'm from the projects in the Southside of Richmond, and we protect our own," Iesha stated, squeezing my hand to make me know she meant that.

I'd always known that women spoke more than one language, and I felt like that was happening in this moment. It sounded like Carmen was saying 'bitch he's mine' and Iesha was saying 'but we're more than friends.' It felt like the two of them were dancing with each other and I didn't like that.

"Iesha, can you give us a minute?" I asked. She squeezed my hand again before letting go and leaving the room.

"You fucking her, Zayvion?" Carmen asked as soon as the door closed.

"Are you being serious right now?"

"You goddamn right! That bitch is a little too friendly to just be your mule, standing by your bedside holding your hand and crying. You fucking that bitch and…"

"Right, because it's just impossible for her to give a fuck about me any other way. There's no way she could be over-whelmed with emotions and just happy that a nigga didn't get stabbed to death. In case you weren't paying attention I almost died!"

"I'm not saying she can't feel some type of way, but she…"

"Carmen, stop! I'm lying in a hospital bed and you wanna have this dumb ass conversation. We're friends, get over it, and while you're doing that go get my daughter."

"What?"

"You heard me. I'm not trying to talk to you while you're on your bullshit, so will you please go get Ariel," I said, letting her hand go. The anger in her face was apparent, but I could see she was thinking better of unleashing it.

"I'll be back," she said, reluctantly leaving my bedside. I needed a few deep breaths after she was gone to steady myself, but sooner than expected my hospital room door swung back open.

"Now that was awkward," Alexis said, laughing.

"Haha, laugh at my pain."

"Hey, you did this to yourself, but it seems like you man-aged to wiggle out of it with your head on your shoulders."

"No, thanks to you, you hauled ass the first chance you got."

"I'm sorry, I don't do messy. Besides I didn't wanna be a witness to any crime committed in this room."

"That's so nice of you," I replied sarcastically.

"Don't be mad at me, it was your dick that got you into this."

"What can I say, it's good dick," I said laughing. That bright red blush was back creepin' across her beautiful face.

"Do you disagree?"

"Disagree with what?" she asked.

"First of all, why are you way over there? Come sit down," I urged. She did as I suggested, but I could tell she was tense.

"So, Alexis, back to my question."

"What was your question again?" It took me a minute to reply because I was fighting off the laughter trying to spring from my throat.

"Is my dick good?" I asked.

"I-I don't know. How would I know that?"

"Are you saying that your sample size was too small?"

"Uh no, it definitely wasn't small," she replied quickly.

"Thank you, but I said your sample size, not the size of it."

"Oh. I guess you could say that."

"We'll just have to fix that, won't we?"

"Zayvion, I…"

"Ah, Mr. Miller, you're awake. How are you feeling?"

"Who are you?" I asked.

"I'm sorry, I'm doctor Cady Mckenzie," she replied.

I saw her mouth moving, but my brain was busy analyzing her beauty. She was maybe five foot two inches tall with short brown hair that matched her hazel eyes nicely. Her lab coat wasn't hiding that figure either.

"I'm feeling okay, Doc, when will I be released?"

"Well, I won't know the answer to that question until I have your test results back. We need to make sure there's no kidney infection, because we did have to go in and close the wound. At the very least you're looking at a couple days here, but I promise you our accommodations are better than where you came from."

"I can't argue with that," I replied.

"I'm just gonna check your vitals really quick."

She did that with a calm swiftness that I was sure put her patients right at ease. The smell of strawberries was heavy on her skin, making me wonder if it would taste the same.

Ordinarily, I might ask or make some suggestive remark, but I already had enough women problems to juggle and to add more would be suicide.

"Seems like you're okay, Mr. Miller, but I'll check on you again later. Try not to move any more than you have to, and order up some room service to help with replenishing your strength," she said, smiling.

"Thanks Doc," I replied, sneaking a glance at the way her lab coat wiggled on her way out.

"Well, I should be going too, I'm sure you'll be having company soon," Alexis said.

"Yeah, I'm waiting on my daughter. Where's Iesha?"

"I think she left, but you know she'll be back when she gets off work."

"What about you, will you be back to visit?"

"Is that what you want?" she asked softly.

"You know the answer to that. I actually want you to take a few days off and spend time with you kids, my treat."

"Zayvion, I can't…"

"Haven't you learned how useless it is to argue with me? Give me your number so I can tell you where to pick up some money, and I want you to take those kids and do something nice. Got it?"

"Whatever you say," she replied, taking a piece of paper out and writing her number down.

"I told you I got you."

"Not yet you don't," she said, winking as she put the number in my hand before heading out the door.

She was definitely a challenge, but I liked that in a woman. I could tell that whatever it was gonna be with her it wouldn't be built on sex or lies. She'd been to that movie and knew how it ended.

Some dudes might've seen that as a cause for concern or a reason to run away, but they weren't looking for a real woman. Considering the fact that I was married to one woman, while having a baby by another, I probably shouldn't have been looking at any women sideways. Just because I had good sense didn't mean I always used it though. I lay there thinking about Carmen versus Iesha versus Alexis until Carmen showed up with my baby girl. I didn't dare tell her that I'd been stabbed. It freaked her out enough to just see me in a hospital bed hooked up like jumper cables.

All she knew was her daddy was sick, but I was getting better and I'd be home soon. When she crawled into the bed with me and went to sleep, Carmen and I discussed the conversation she had with my lawyer about whether or not to postpone my trial date. Tomorrow morning, he was going to file the motion to try and get me home on house arrest. Given the fact that I'd been assaulted by an unknown person, my chances were at a fifty-fifty chance. I didn't wanna push my court date back if I couldn't get the house arrest. I wanted to get the fuck out of prison A.S.A.P. The look on her face and the tears in her eyes said we were in agreement, even though we didn't talk about the argument we'd had earlier.

We enjoyed our time together until the Doctor came back in and said I needed to get some rest. Thankfully, Ariel was still asleep or there would've been a fight to get her out of bed with me. Carmen agreed to bring her back tomorrow, and after I told her about the money I wanted to give to Alexis they left. I tried to just relax and clear my mind, but that proved to be harder to do in a hospital than it was in prison. I mean there was literally death all around me and that wasn't a soothing thought.

After an hour of staring at the ceiling, I called Carmen to make sure she got home safe and that she'd Western Union the money to Alexis. I thought she might ask me a million questions about the money, but apparently, her focus had been too distracted by Iesha to find out who the other girl in the room had been. Still our conversation seemed strained, so I ended it before it got to the periods of awkward silence. I tried to sleep, but that shit was as elusive as my release date. Finally, I picked up the phone and called Alexis. When she answered, I didn't get a word in for the first three minutes, while she told me that I had no business sending her a thousand dollars.

I'd never known a woman to take offense to money, but part way through our conversation I understood that it might look like I was trying to buy her. This realization led me to explain my appreciation for the grind of a single mother so she would understand that I was only trying to help. Granted this was abnormal behavior for most men, so it took some convincing before she agreed to take a couple days off and spoil her kids. With the business out of the way we just fell into a rhythm and kicked it. Hours passed and more times than I wanted to admit I had to breathe through the pain of laughter, but I still didn't wanna get off the phone.

Eventually, we had no choice though, because being a single mom wasn't just something that looked good on paper. For the next day and a half, I spent more time on the phone with Alexis than anyone else. Carmen and Iesha both came to see me, thankfully at different times, but I was honestly looking forward to seeing Alexis again. When my lawyer showed up on my third day in the hospital I had to put the thought of all women to the side because shit was real. The judge had denied my motion for house arrest, but that wasn't even the tip of the iceberg of bad news. Apparently, the remaining witnesses against me had second thoughts about their testimony, which worked in my favor, but the judge held them all in contempt and now they were screaming to tell all they knew.

There still was no word on who the CI was, and when my lawyer had sent someone into the areas where the drugs were caught, my name was ringing like Pablo Escobar's! The only good news he had was that Carmen's whereabouts were accounted for on the days when the busts happened. So basically, they had to prove I was the dope man and all they had was hearsay, but I had even less, because the courts were known to believe the mufuckas that talked. In the end, I didn't even have to ask my lawyer what my best plan of action was because it was obvious the witnesses needed to go away. Of course, that would make the courts look harder at me, but if they couldn't prove shit then it didn't matter. I was starting to feel like Al Capone, and nobody could tell me who I could or couldn't kill, but first I had to find out who the CI was.

I made sure my lawyer knew to get in touch with the warden and let him know that I didn't know who stabbed me, I wouldn't tolerate being thrown in protective custody or under investigation without filing a lawsuit, and I wasn't gonna retaliate. Right now, my mission was to get back around David and wait for his mom to come through with the information I needed. It's hard to fight an enemy I couldn't see, but now I knew someone wanted me dead I could take the necessary steps to protect myself. It was simple really. I supplied two of the main organizations on both sides of the prison, so somebody fucking with me was somebody taking food out their mouths. Starving niggas didn't come off their lunch money, and a lion never missed a meal. All I had to do was play the game and *win*.

Chapter Sixteen

I'd spent almost a week flat on my back and the doctor had said I'd probably experience some soreness because of that. Being sore was better than being dead though.

"I heard you might be released into the wild today."

"Well, look who finally found the time to come and see me. How are you, Daniels?"

"Ms. Daniels? So, official now."

"I'm just fucking with you. How have you been, Alexis?"

"I'm good. And I would've been here sooner, but someone insisted that I take a few days off and spend time with my children."

"Did you have fun?" I asked, adjusting my bed into a sitting position. I was still in pain, but it seemed like the worst of it had passed.

"Yes, I did have fun. Thank you."

"No need to thank me, you already saved my life."

"Speaking of which, what happens when you get back to prison?" she asked, taking a seat in the chair next to my bed.

"What do you mean?"

"I mean, obviously whoever tried to kill you is gonna be disappointed that they didn't get the job done. And from what you told me I know you're determined to go right back to general population. What happens if or when they come at you again?"

"I'll just have to be ready."

"What does that mean, Zayvion?"

"It means I'll have my eyes open and be ready to protect myself."

"Can you grow eyes in the back of your head too?" she asked sarcastically.

"My niggas got my back."

"Who can you really trust though?"

"What do you want me to say, Alexis? Prison ain't for nice guys. It's the belly of the beast and only the strong survive. You know as well as I do that stabbings and violence come with the territory."

"Exactly, and that's why I don't think you should be walking back into the situation right now."

"Well, sweetheart, I would love to go home, but that's not my call at the moment. What else can I do? Go into protective custody?"

"Is that so bad? I'd get to see you and I'd make sure you are taken care of," she said.

Her words sounded sincere to me and I liked that, because most people in her situation didn't give a fuck. I still couldn't do what she wanted.

"As much as I appreciate the offer, I can't go to protective custody, but I'll be protected."

"Zayvion, you don't know that! You said yourself that you don't know who it was that stabbed you, so it could be someone you consider a friend."

The truth in her words hung between us, and I couldn't deny that she might be right. I'd lost track of the hours I'd spent trying to figure out who wanted me dead, but so far all I'd been able to come up with was it possibly being a friend of Big T. I'd already decided that Hambone had never sent for me to come to breakfast, so if I could find out who the messenger was then maybe I'd know who set me up. I didn't think it was anyone I truly fucked with, but I'd be willfully ignorant to overlook the playgrounds I was playing in.

"I admit that you could be right. Do you worry about all your patients like this?" I asked, smiling.

"You know you're way more than a patient to me, but don't try to change the subject. I'm worried about you."

"I can see that and I appreciate it. But you're causing yourself unnecessary gray hair."

"I do not have gray hair!" she exclaimed, slapping me on my leg.

"You will if you keep worrying. You'll start to get lines and shit on your face, and you'll look old before your time."

"I'll still look good though," she replied smiling.

"I won't argue with you about that. Listen, I'm gonna level with you, because you've earned my trust, given what we've went through. I have to be in population right now, because I'm fighting for my freedom."

"What do you mean?" she asked.

I ran my legal trouble down for her and explained how bad it could get, but I didn't mention David or the strings his mom was pulling. She took all the information in with a straight face, but I could see the analyzing going on behind her eyes. No one could really understand what it's like to fight for your life, but those who cared for you could feel that pain of loss. Looking at Alexis I realized how much everything had changed between us in just a matter of days.

We'd fast tracked a friendship only to end up in a world of our own I couldn't really categorize, but I definitely appreciated it.

"Wow," she said.

"What does that mean?"

"It's just...I mean you've got a lot going on in your life right now."

"That's an understatement."

"Yeah it is. I just didn't realize all you were dealing with," she said, taking my hand. Her fingers were soft and warm as they laced with mine, and I loved the way our hands fit together.

"I've thought about this," I said.

"About what?"

"Us holding hands. I know it's an innocent gesture, but to me it's an intimate expression that's overlooked these days. I remember when I was younger it was a big deal to hold a girl's hand."

"I bet you held a lot of hands," she said smiling.

"I was a cute kid!"

"I can believe that," she replied, looking at our joined hands.

I tugged on her hand gently until she was standing over me and then I pulled her down into my arms for a kiss. She tasted like peppermints and her lips were as soft and juicy as I remembered. I took my time with her, wanting to make sure the exploration of her mouth was a mission of thoroughness. She gave as good as she got, bringing our tongues and lips together like the perfect beat and an unforgettable hook that could do nothing less than make your head nod. Our kisses were mind blowing, but I wanted more. I knew there was a risk of someone coming in and catching us, but that made it more exciting.

Using my free hand, I pulled my blanket back and then I pulled her onto my lap, thankful for the jean skirt she was wearing. She straddled me willingly, taking my face in her hands to let me know she was capable of taking control when needed. I fumbled with the buttons to adjust the bed, letting it down a little until we were in a reclined position. Once that was accomplished, I put my hands back to good use under her skirt, pulling her panties aside and moving my gown until there was only air between what we wanted.

"I don't wanna hurt you," she whispered.

"We'll go slow," I replied, grabbing her hips and guiding her downward gently.

The heat coming from her pussy was incredible and the moment I broke her threshold I was lost. She sat down on my dick achingly slow, looking me in the eyes the whole time and letting me watch her hunger build. When she backed up our faces were only inches apart and I could hear the moan of need start way down in her throat. Her pussy was tighter than I remembered, and it felt so good that I had to remind myself to breathe when she took all of me inside her again.

"You feel so damn good, baby," I murmured.

"I've been saving it," she rasped into my ear before biting my neck hard.

The shock she sent through my body was pure electricity, and it ripped a growl from my throat. With my hand still on her hips, I pulled her down harder, ignoring the screams from my back because I needed the good feeling more.

"Easy, baby, I got you," she whispered into my ear, swiveling her hips as she set our rhythm to a slow gallop.

All I could do was hold on as she rose and fell, rose and fell, molding our bodies into synchronized ecstasy. Never before had I given up total control, but with Alexis astride me nothing felt more right. She came without warning the first time, damn near pushing me over the edge with her, but I held on and pushed up into her as she rained on me. The way her body quivered had her pussy squeezing my dick and the feeling was beyond my ability to describe it.

"I need all of you," I told her.

"I'm g-giving it to you," she vowed, moving faster, chasing her next orgasm.

The struggle was real, so real in fact that we didn't hear the door open until it was too late.

"Oh! I'm s-sorry!" I heard a woman's voice say, her voice freezing us both in place.

"W-who was that?" Alexis panted.

"Doctor."

"W-we gotta stop," she said, but even as the words were coming out of her mouth, she was moving again taking us higher.

"Oh shit," I moaned.

"Uh huh, I w-want you to cum with me," she said, pumping her hips faster and taking my dick inside her as far as I could go.

Our mouths found each other with the passion of lost lovers as she took what she wanted and I gave her all I had, until finally neither of us could hold back and we came loudly together.

"That was…that was…"

"I know," she replied laying her head on my shoulder, trying to catch her breath.

I'd known her pussy was good from our first encounter, but I had no idea that it would be hands down the best I ever had! My dick was still inside her and I never wanted to take it out, but us getting caught like that had me paranoid.

"Did the doctor see when you came in?"

"No, I don't think so. Why?"

"Because I don't want her calling the prison if she recognizes you," I said.

"I doubt she would, I mean I'm wearing street clothes and my hair is down. You didn't comment on how different I look either," she said, jabbing me in the chest with her finger.

"You're absolutely gorgeous."

"You wouldn't just be saying that because a very important part of you is inside me, would you?"

"Of course not. I've always thought you were a gorgeous woman."

"Good answer," she said kissing me quickly before climbing off me.

"Aww, why'd you move?"

"Because we don't want anyone else to walk in on us, and you know I'm right so put that thing away," she instructed, eyeing my dick like she was trying to etch it into her memory.

I made sure to wag it at her before putting my gown down, which made her laugh on her way to the bathroom to clean up. I hadn't needed any more women problems to complete my life, but I knew for sure I'd just walked into one. Not that Alexis was drama, because I knew she wasn't, just like I knew I couldn't only live with just a taste of her. I needed hours, days, years to appreciate and learn her body until I could call it my own.

Deep down I knew these weren't the thoughts of a married man, but somewhere inside me I could hear a voice saying 'fuck all that, keep her around.' And maybe it was because I knew that things between Carmen and I might not go right if my trial didn't. Maybe it was because no matter how the movie ended I didn't see me and Iesha moving off into the sunset together. Whatever it was, shit was definitely different between Alexis and I, and I was committed to exploring it until it's end.

"You okay?" I asked once she came out of the bathroom.

"I'm good. Actually, I'm better than good, but I don't want that to go to your head."

"With the way you just worked me, I wouldn't dream of being cocky," I replied smiling.

"Somehow I think you'll return the favor."

"So this wasn't just a one time thing for you?" I asked.

"I'm not into one night stands, Zay. I don't know what'll happen in the future because of everything you have going on, but I felt it was okay to share this moment."

"You didn't really answer my question."

"Zayvion...I don't want it to be a one time thing, but I don't know what I should want or expect from you. Your life is complicated, and I mean that just from the females in it. Do you really have room for me?"

"I'll make room. No matter what happens I'm gonna be in your life, so why don't we figure it out as we go along?"

"I guess that's all we can do," she replied.

"Miller, your vacation is over," a CO said coming through the door, dangling the travel jewelry of handcuffs, a waist chain and the dreaded black box.

"We even brought you a brand-new jumpsuit," a second CO said coming through the door behind the first.

"What are you doing here, Daniels?" the first CO asked.

"I came to examine him before transport, that way if anything was wrong, the institution won't get the blame," she replied. I smiled at her, admiring how quick she was on her feet.

"Thank you, Nurse Daniels," I said.

"No problem, Miller, I'll see you back at the prison." Noticing that the COs were solely focused on me, she winked and blew me a kiss on her way out the door, which kept a smile on my face as I maneuvered into the Khaki colored jumpsuit.

Once I was dressed, one CO went to get my doctor while the other assembled the rest of my wardrobe on me.

"Ah, Mr. Miller. I'm sorry for my earlier interruption, but it's good to see that you've healed rather nicely," she said, giving me a smile that only the two of us understood.

"I'm feeling okay, Doc, but I know you're probably gonna tell me to refrain from heavy lifting."

"Indeed. I've also prescribed you some things to make sure your kidney function is normal, and the medical staff at the institution will monitor you and change your bandages."

"Okay. Thanks, Doc."

"No problem, just try not to fall on anybody's knife again, because you might not be so lucky."

Once the other CO came in with the wheelchair we loaded up and begin the journey back to the thunder dome. Going back to prison would ordinarily have a mufucka depressed as all hell, but I was hopeful that I had good things awaiting me. I wasn't worried about whoever stabbed me, because Iesha and I had already set a plan in motion. For the right price, anybody could get touched, and I was definitely gonna make the price right for whoever had come for me.

I wasn't just gonna touch him though, I was gonna touch the people he cared about and set an example for anyone else who might have any ideas. I was hopeful that I'd be going home soon, but if I wasn't and prison was to be my new home then I damn sure wasn't doing day for day looking over my shoulder. I had too much money for that and money meant power and power invoked fear where respect was lacking. Once I was secured back behind the razor wire, I was taken to medical and evaluated for real this time by old nurse Doris. What should've taken a matter of minutes lasted damn near an hour, which had me stuck sitting in medical through count time.

I used that time to get my mind right and adjust my thoughts to fit my environment. I still had the scent of Alexis on my skin, but I knew I couldn't climb into those memories until I was alone and I could let my guard down.

"Mr. Miller." I looked up to find the warden standing in front of me.

"Warden Cook," I said.

"Miller, it's against my better judgment to put you back in general population, but you somehow managed to circumvent my arguments. You may think that's a good thing, but I've seen this place chew up bigger and badder mufuckas than you. With that being said, you need to sign this, because I'm damn sure gonna cover my ass," he said, handing me a piece of paper.

A quick look at what I was holding revealed it to be a waiver that took all liability off of the administration for my choice to go back to population. I read it quickly and then looked up into the smug look on his leathered white face. I could tell he expected me not to sign it and to change my mind about going back to my normal housing now that it was imminent. He had me fucked up.

"Got a pen?" I asked. I signed the paper quickly and returned it to him.

"When count clears send him upstairs," he said to the CO who was stationed in front of medical.

I only had to wait another five minutes, for that to happen, and when it did I was on the move without hesitation.

"What's up, Ms. G?" I asked once I'd gotten to my floor.

"Hey boy! It's good to see you still walking around."

"You know I ain't going down without a fight."

"I heard that. I'm bout to open all the cells now and I know there's gonna be a party tonight."

"I couldn't have it any other way, but you know you're invited," I said, winking at her.

"Boy, you're crazy," she replied, laughing and turning the knobs to open the front gate along with the doors to all the cells.

"Next time make sure you hit me with a proper banger, bitch!"

I screamed for everyone to hear. Niggas poured out of their cells to see what was happening and when they saw me cheers erupted like we were at the NBA finals. I got hugs from mufuckas I didn't even know, but my niggas pushed them all to the side to make sure I was alright. They were happy to see me, but they wanted the niggas head responsible for what happened. I was getting ready to lay out my plan for the day back when I saw David signaling for me.

"What is it?" I asked once I got to the door.

"My mom has what you need."

Aryanna

Chapter Seventeen

The joy I felt at hearing these words damn near made up for the stabbing I'd taken.

"Don't play with me," I warned him.

"I'm not. She wouldn't tell me what the information was, because she wants to talk to you. But she's got it, I promise."

"Okay, when should I call her?"

"She had to go to New York on business, but she's supposed to be back tomorrow. You can try her then," he replied.

"Cool. Is everything good with you?"

"Yeah, Leslie has been looking out for me, and nobody has bothered me."

"That's good. I'll holla at you after I get myself settled," I told him, noticing my cousin motioning for me to come to the cell. When I walked in it was packed with Boo Gotti, Double Oh and Fred already seated.

"What's shakin,' my dudes?" I asked, closing the door and covering the window.

Ham gave me a hug that was so heartfelt I thought he might start crying, but instead he backed up and passed me a cigar.

"Damn, I gotta roll the blunt now?" I asked.

"Nah, nigga, that mufucka is packed tight with the green, just light it," Boo Gotti said passing me a torch. I hit it hard enough to choke the first time, but I still didn't pass it.

"So what's up? Y'all miss me?"

"Yo, what happened, Zay?" Fred asked.

I knew they were all happy to see me, but the look on their faces was all business. I ran it down to them from the beginning, and I could already see Ham shaking his head saying he never sent for me. Boo Gotti and his goons had been asking questions, not so quietly, while I was gone, but they were

157

getting mixed answers. Some niggas were saying it was about my putting a hit on Big T, but others were saying the hit came from the streets with a price tag attached.

"Who would want you dead out there?" Ham asked.

He knew as well as I did that list could have a lot of names on it, especially given what I was going through right now. For all I know the nigga Capel could've put a hit on me for the threats I'd sent him. A rule I'd learned long ago was you never threatened a nigga. That was just giving him a chance to act before you did. I should've either killed Capel or left him alone, but I'd let my feelings affect my judgment. I couldn't make that mistake again.

"Listen, we all know that the penitentiary has no secrets, so eventually this shit is gonna come to light and be exposed. Right now, all eyes are on me because of the administration not wanting to put me back in population so soon. We know that bringing heat doesn't make money. So, what I suggest is we get back to the money until we know exactly what happened and why, and then when the time is right it'll be handled. Revenge is so sweet because you get to serve it up on your own time, just when the other person is comfortable in their own skin."

"Well, from now on we got you, and the word is out to all my homies across the state, no matter where you go," Boo Gotti said.

"My uncle did the same thing." Fred chimed in.

"I appreciate the love. So, what's up, we gonna party or what?"

That was the wrong question for me to ask because it was a full two hours before I stumbled out of my cell higher than Snoop Dogg had ever been! I stopped counting after the third blunt we smoked, but them mufuckas wasn't regular blunts. We had to rename them the body snatchers. On top of that I must've snorted every bit of a gram of coke, but I chalked it up to coming so close to death that I had to enjoy life every now and then. I don't know whose bright idea it was to crank up the poker table, but all of a sudden we were all sitting around like a scene from good fellas.

At some point, I heard that Jeezy 101 bumping from somebody's speakers, causing everybody to nod to the feel created by dope boy music. There was absolutely no substitute for being home, but it felt good when we could make the best out of a bad situation.

"Leslie!" I hollered.

"I'm already cooking, nigga, just keep playing cards," he replied.

I laughed at that. When they called pill call I signaled Ham to follow me. Part of it was that I needed help with the work, but the other part was that I wasn't stupid enough to travel by myself knowing I wasn't a hundred percent. If a nigga will try you when you strong then he'll definitely do it when you weak. As soon as we bent the corner by medical I spotted Iesha holding up the doorway. When she saw us she motioned for us to come on, saying something to the CO at the desk that we were too far away too hear.

She told him that Trish would call him out in a second and she took me to a room in the back. As soon as the door was closed she was in my arms kissing me fiercely.

"I missed you so fucking much! You don't know, Zay. And I'm sorry about the shit with Carmen and…"

"Slow down, Iesha. I accepted your apologies the first time and I told you we were good."

"I know, baby, but things ain't been the same between us," she replied panting.

I could tell her that was because I had Alexis on my mind, but that would be the dumbest shit in the world for me to say. Instead I wanted to get to business.

"Listen, I might know who the CI's ID testifying against me."

"Who?"

"I'm waiting on confirmation, but I should know tomorrow."

"And then what?"

"And then I want your dude, Shmurda, to handle that."

"But I thought you said that was making shit hot?" she asked.

"I might not come home any other way."

That thought put tears in her eyes instantly and she clung to me tighter. I held her and stroked her back for a few minutes, but I felt a tremor of panic when she started unbuttoning my jumpsuit. Even though I was high out of my mind, I still knew my dick was dirty from me and Alexis earlier, and if this woman smelled another on me then shit was gonna hit the fan.

"Baby, what are you doing?" I asked.

"I need you."

"We don't have time."

"We'll make time," she replied, still popping my buttons on her way down. The only thing I could think to do was play offense, so I spun her around and pulled her pants and panties to the floor.

"Baby, wait, I wanna suck your dick first," she said.

There was no way in hell I could let that happen, so I ignored her protests while bending her over and ramming my dick inside her. That definitely shut her up until I started pounding her into orgasmic shock. As soon as she came I pulled out of her and let her finish me off the way she'd wanted to start, burying my dick deep in her throat while she swallowed every drop.

"Damn, I guess you did miss me," I said, trying to catch my breath and regain my balance.

"I told you that. I got something for you," she said opening a drawer and pulling out a paper lunch bag.

"Five ounces?" I asked.

"Yeah, the coke and the heroin are marked differently. Did you really need that much?"

"I gotta make the necessary moves, babe, you know that."

"Okay. Speaking of which, I want you to call or text me as soon as you find out who the CI is. I'ma hit my people up and make sure everything is ready."

"Thanks, sweetheart," I said, pulling her towards me for a kiss.

It was crazy, but I swore I could taste Alexis's pussy along with our own sex on her tongue. I tucked the sack she gave me into my underwear, buttoned up my jumpsuit, and then stood back for her to inspect me.

"I can't see it," she said.

"Good. How much money do you got put away for when the baby comes?"

"A little over eight thousand dollars I think."

"Okay. It's time to start thinking about a house too, because you'll be well over a hundred thousand dollars in a few days."

"I'll start looking and get with my mother to put it in her name."

"Cool. I'll call you," I said, kissing her and leaving out.

I found him sitting in the waiting area where I'd left him and he shook his head to let me know he'd made his pick up too.

"What took you so long?" he asked once we were in the hallway headed back to our floor.

"She gets what she wants."

"Damn, why her homegirl be faking then?"

"What you mean?" I asked.

"She ain't let me get up in them guts yet!"

"Maybe she ain't feeling your demo, or maybe you ain't coming out of pocket for that extra attention. Feel me?"

"Man, whatever. I'll throw her a few dollars, but she need to get with the program," he said.

We made it back to our floor safely and I sent him in so I could have a word with Ms. G real quick.

"Ms. G, can I holla at you?"

"What you need?"

"Listen, I need a favor. I'm 'bout to pull an all nighter and I can't afford to have nobody run down on my cell. I just need everything to be real quiet up here, and I got you."

"What you mean you got me?" she asked.

"Stop past my cell when you lockdown."

"Okay."

With that piece of business out of the way, I went straight to my cell to put my stash away.

"What you got?" I asked Ham once the door was closed.

"Two ounces of coke and two of that horse, plus the cash you wanted."

I counted the hundred dollar bills quickly and then folded them up as small as I could get them before putting them in my pocket.

"You got the baking soda?" I asked, pulling my own package out and separating the coke from the heroin. He reached under the bed and pulled out a big ass bag.

"It's gonna be a long night, how much weed you got?"

"Boo Gotti hit this time, go holla at him," he replied.

"Let's get the little shit out of the way that way I can holla at everybody while I'm out there."

We quickly put together a few grams, and then I hit the floor making my rounds. You'd have thought I was the second coming of Christ with how happy mufuckas were to see me back in action. Once I'd reached everybody I needed to and

162

traded Boo for some of that sticky I was back in my cell waiting on lockdown to come. A few minutes ahead of schedule Ms. G hit the floor and I told Ham to step out real quick. I knew she could be bought, but I still wasn't stupid enough to have dope scattered all over the place in front of her, so I made sure my work space was covered.

She went straight to the ice machine, and that's when I called her over to tell her about my toilet being stopped up. When she stepped in the cell I passed her the money, and she stepped back out I watched her as she went back into the booth and sat down, directly counting the money where no one could see. When she looked up our eyes locked and she shook her head to let me know we were straight. I signaled Ham to come back to the cell.

"Let's get to work," I said, separating a line of coke a piece for us.

Neither of us would know sleep tonight because between the two of us we had nine ounces, but by morning it would be scrambled into eighteen/twenty. Then we were gonna hit both sides of the prison, and reach out to the surrounding institutions on the farm, like a blizzard. It was a risky move to make for sure, but it would bring the results I wanted in the form of answers to what happened to me, and the loyalty that's so often purchased behind the wall. It wasn't a money play, even though we stood to hit six figures easily. This is about showing the difference between me being around and me not being around, this was establishing value.

"You ready?" I asked, once Ms. G had come back around to lock and check the doors.

"Roll the weed and don't fuck up the cut," he said.

I didn't know how good the heroin was, but the coke was certified, which meant it would survive being stepped on big time. We worked slowly, methodically, only taking breaks to smoke a blunt or toke a line and then it was back to business. I made the mistake of distracting myself by texting Alexis to see how her night was going and before I knew it we were on the phone kickin' it. She was so easy to talk to and laugh with, but Ham interrupted by complaining that he was doing all the work.

Reluctantly, I got off the phone, and that's when I noticed I had a voicemail. When I checked it, I was surprised to hear David's mom insisting that I call her no matter what time it was, day or night. I figured it could wait until morning, but the more I thought about it, the more curious I was so I called her. There wasn't a hint of sleep in her voice, and the immediate topic of conversation was her son. She could appreciate that I was looking out for him, but she wanted to know what would happen if something happened to me.

Given my recent hospital run I could understand her worry, but I gave her a brief rundown on how shit worked behind the wall and I explained David would be good regardless. I could still feel her worry through the phone, but as a parent I could understand it. She was a woman of her word though, because she'd dug into my case, but given the way three witnesses had gone to meet Jesus she was nervous about giving me any information. I didn't have to break it down for her though because at the end of the day none of their lives were worth her son's. The remaining seven witnesses were sequestered in a hotel in Philly under the protection of the commonwealth of Pennsylvania.

As for the CI, he was still out operating, but when she finally revealed his name I thought she was joking. I did my best to explain that there was no way she had accurate information, but she proved me wrong by sending me pictures of the paperwork he signed to solidify his cooperation.

"What's up, nigga, you look like you've seen a ghost," Ham said.

"It's worse than that. I know who set me up now, but I don't know why."

Aryanna

Chapter Eighteen

I moved on autopilot through the rest of the night, trying to understand what the fuck was going on and how this came to be reality. The more I thought about it though the more sense it made why the government was cocky enough to offer me a plea deal of fifty years. They had everything they needed to bury me. The more time that passed, the more that really started to sink in. I was looking down the barrel of forever unless I took their deal, or I made a deal myself. I couldn't do that though, because the snitch was basically putting the gun to the heads of everybody I loved and pulling the trigger.

I was down to my last two options and one of them had to work. Hour after hour until the sun came up I tried to call Rocko, but I got no answer. I needed to call Carmen, but I wasn't ready for that conversation until I had a game plan. I knew my wife and if I told her too much she was gonna go straight at the nigga with complete disregard for her safety. I couldn't put her in harms way like that. As soon as I knew Iesha was off the clock I sent her all the information I had, making it clear that shit needed to be handled immediately. For the moment that was my only play, which meant I had to sit back and wait with the patience of a death row inmate who hoped the governor would call in time to stop the execution.

When our door was unlocked, me and Ham got to work like we were trapping in the streets, only putting seven ounces in the stash spot. The only niggas I did hand to hand with on the weight was Boo Gotti and Fred. It was their responsibility to reach everybody else and make sure the money was right when they did business. After I made my moves I took a much needed shower and then went right back in my cell to wait on the money to come through. Within the hour I was getting texts from all over with green dot numbers and amounts, and I had to handle my part of the business by forwarding the information to Carmen and Iesha. Within the first three days we cleared a hundred thousand dollars, acquired some important favors, and found out the hit on me did come from the streets.

Even knowing that, Big T's homeboys still got fucked up, in case they were thinking of some type of retaliation against me. Finally, knowing who the mufucka was that was set to testify against me put my stabbing and the price tag that came with it into perspective. He was smart enough to know that once I found out I'd put a price on his head too, and that was an easier job in the street. I use to know all his hiding spots, but these days nobody could give me an answer on his whereabouts. It was looking like he'd gone underground. With my trial date only days away, and since he was in the streets, not even David's mom could provide me with a location.

My options were running out. Iesha had her people on the hunt, but it was like looking for a needle in a haystack, because he could literally be anywhere. All I knew for certain was where his bitch ass was gonna be on the day I was set to stand trial, but only a crazy person would hit somebody at the courthouse. I wasn't B. Sigel and this wasn't a movie. As the day drew nearer I felt the pressure mounting as visions of my future behind bars became clearer. I was trying not to panic, but each day with no sighting of the CI was making me physically sick! Carmen still didn't know the truth, I mean there was just no way to put it to her and keep her on the sidelines.

I had enough to worry about with Iesha's crazy ass, because the fact that the other witnesses were heavily guarded had her losing her damn mind. I feared she might try to handle the situation herself and go in dressed like a maid, guns blazing. Alexis was my only avenue of sanity, but we were both feeling some type of way about not seeing each other. It wasn't just about the sex, even though it was mind-blowing, we really just wanted to spend some time together. It only took two all-night conversations before I came up with the idea of getting Iesha to take a day off, and that only left the obstacle of Alexis making sure she worked that shift. When I got called down to medical right before lockdown I knew it had all worked out.

"Why am I going to medical, Ms. G?"

"Your guess is as good as mine, but I'll walk you down there since I'm going on break anyway."

Nobody moved after count without an escort, now I just had to hope the CO downstairs was cool.

"You know you didn't have to give me that much," Ms. G whispered once we were in the stairway.

"What do you mean?"

"I know it was you who told Boo to step his game up. I see how you move, and when he came out of nowhere and started giving me money I knew you were behind that,"

"I don't know what you are talking about," I replied smiling.

"Boy, please, I'm not complaining. I wanted to give him some pussy just because I respect how he moves and he's always made sure I was respected. This job is real life, I mean every day I put my life on the line, but I feel safe when I know he's around."

"That's because he won't let shit happen to you."

"I don't believe you would either. All I'm saying is I appreciate you rubbing off on him, you're not a bad guy."

"Thank you," I replied, genuinely surprised by her comment.

Our conversation became less personal as we made our way to medical, you never knew what the ears of other COs were trying to pick up. They told on each other as much as inmates did. She escorted me to medical, and the CO at the desk looked like she could care less how long I was in medical because it was her lunchtime.

"Mr. Miller, I'm gonna change your bandages," Alexis said, leading me into an exam room. Once we were behind closed doors we stood there staring at each other, almost like we were unsure of what to do.

"I've missed you," I said.

"It's good to be missed. I missed you too."

"Then why are you way over there?"

"I could ask you the same thing," she replied smiling.

Crossing to her I took her in my arms and kissed her, showing her just how much I'd missed being in her presence. I was ready to take it there, but we needed to talk, because I hadn't exactly been honest with her in recent conversations.

"I go to court in a few days," I said, pulling back a little so I could look into her chocolate brown eyes.

"Okay…and?"

"And I know who's gonna testify against me. I know how the feds built their case."

"Is that good or bad?"

"Both. It's only good if I can deal with it before court, but if I can't then…then it's all bad. I might be forced to take a plea."

"For how long?" she asked just above a whisper.

"They offered me fifty."

"Fifty? Fifty years? Zayvion, there's no way you can take that deal, I mean you'd be seventy-five when you got out!"

"I know. I don't have a lot of options, Alexis."

"Any option is better than that one, so tell me what the alternatives are."

"Escape," I said. The word hung between us for a moment and I could see her doing the math in her eyes.

"If you need my help…"

"You know you can't."

"But I…"

"Sweetheart, we can't go on the run with three kids, and I'd think less of you if you offered to leave them for a little while. There are no substitutions or replacements for a mother's love, babe."

When the tears began filling her eyes I knew she understood the truth I spoke, but she didn't argue with it. I hated to see the pain I was causing her, but through that pain came something I hadn't expected to see. I saw a possible future for us.

"What if…what if I told you there was one other way, but it would mean that you'd have to leave everything you knew behind?"

"What do you mean?"

"We wouldn't be running from the law, but we would still have to relocate. Could you see yourself starting over with me?"

"What about my kids? What about your kids and your wife and your baby mama?"

"Carmen and I would be through, and Iesha and I can co-parent. As for your kids, you should know by now that I wouldn't be dealing with you without understanding the package deal."

"Wait, so are you telling me there's a way for you to avoid prison altogether?"

"I believe so."

"Then fuck the details, we can worry about that once you're out. Just come home to me."

"Do you mean that?" I asked.

"I do."

"Okay, then I'm gonna need your help. I've got a little money stashed away that no one knows about and I want you to go get it."

"Once I do that what's the plan?"

I ran down to her what was needed and how things would go once I was out. We worked out the details while she changed the bandage on my back, and by the time she was done I was at peace with my decision. This was a dog eat dog world and there was no way I could allow myself to go out like a bitch in heat. When I finally went to sleep that night, I did so knowing that I'd played the game trusting my instincts and using strategy. I spent the next couple of days laying the groundwork, meeting with both my PO and my lawyer to topple the dominos towards my freedom.

Naturally, my PO was pissed, but my lawyer found the whole thing amusing and he actually asked if I was clairvoyant. I told him sadly I wasn't, it was just the nature of the streets to try and expect the unexpected when you were bout that life. There was no need to postpone my court date, because the days leading to it would be used to put the pieces together, which left me doing the same thing on the inside. I couldn't tell everybody that I was chasing my freedom, because nobody really knew what I was going through except Ham.

No matter where I was in the world I had to make sure my niggas were taken care of for as long as they were in this situation. The night before my trial began, I brought my dudes together and finally told them what I'd been dealing with for the last couple of months. They all understood why I'd kept my cards close, but they wished me the best, and we put several blunts in the air in salute of keeping it real, despite how the game had changed. No matter how far away I got on the outside I knew I'd never forget the inside because of niggas like these.

The things you experience in this type of hell can bond you for life, because no one who hadn't walked these miles can know how these shoes fit. Prison isn't what you saw in the movies, it was deeper than that. I learned that lesson through experiences, but I wasn't willing to give my life to it. I didn't get any sleep once lockdown came. I spent the night smoking blunt after blunt talking to Alexis about our plans. I wasn't sure if what we had was love, but both of us were willing to find out. I still didn't have a solid solution on what to do about Iesha, I was moving one step at a time through a mine field.

At dawn, I stuffed a cigar full of weed and chased it with two lines of blow up my nose, hoping that would be enough to get my mind right. It was a little after seven a.m. when I was called downstairs and I was laced with my favorite jewelry. The whole ride to the courthouse I watched the world around me, knowing that I would soon be part of it again. The question after that was what I'd do next. I was getting ready to change the game and that might shut some doors that had been open my entire life. I could see a future, but I couldn't see the future. It was too late to unwring the bell now though. It was time for show and tell.

"Alright, Miller, let's go," the CO said, opening the car door and helping me out.

We took the same path travelled last time through the back door and straight into the elevator that dropped us off on the second floor. The courtroom had doubled in population, but I was still able to pick Carmen out, dressed to impress in her black suit jacket with the matching skirt and fuck me pumps. She was beautiful and I loved that she was here to support me, but I knew she was about to be heartbroken. As soon as our eyes locked she was smiling and wagging her fingers at me. I smiled back at her, but my attention was immediately pulled to my lawyer who was already sitting at the table with a shit-eating grin on his face.

"You're a goddamn evil genius, you know that?" he said excitedly once I'd sat down next to him.

"I'm glad you think so."

"I'm not the only one either, because the U.S. government has gladly accepted your deal," he said, sliding a piece of paper and pen in front of me.

I read it quickly, amazed that all the pieces of the puzzle had come together the way they had, but thankful that they did. I picked up the pen to sign it, but Carmen's voice stopped me.

"Zay, what's that?" she asked from her seat.

"I'll explain later, babe."

"No, tell me what you're signing."

"It's ok, Carmen, I promise. It's a deal that…"

"You can't sign a deal, Zay!"

"Baby, keep your voice down. It's all good. Trust me."

"Zayvion, you have to come home now. You can't sign a deal, not even to do a day," she said, almost coming over the railing that separated us.

"Carmen, calm the fuck down! You don't understand who was about to testify."

"I don't care! I'm pregnant!"

"All rise, the honorable Judge Valerie Malloy presiding," the bailiff yelled.

My lawyer had to physically pull me to my feet because my brain couldn't function past what Carmen had just blurted out to me. Pregnant? I'd managed to avoid us having sex again after the conversation of her wanting another baby came up, but apparently, she'd got what she wanted that day in the bathroom.

"You may be seated," the Judge said.

My lawyer tapped the paper in front of me and I scribbled my signature across it without a second thought. Carmen was right, one day was too long.

"Case number D-1759321 the United States Federal Court versus Zayvion Miller for two counts of conspiracy to distribute narcotics, namely crack cocaine, methamphetamine and heroin. As well as two counts of illegal weapons trafficking. Mr.

Watkins, are you prepared to give your opening statement at this time?" Judge Malloy asked.

"Uh, Your Honor, may we approach?" my lawyer asked, taking the paper I'd just signed with him.

He handed it to the DA on their way to side bar with the judge and the DA did most of the talking throughout the exchange. The judge looked over the paperwork, asked a couple of questions, and then sent them back to their respective tables.

"It seems that an agreement has been reached between Mr. Miller and the prosecution, but before we get to that I'll ask the bailiff to escort the confidential informant into the courtroom," Judge Malloy said.

You could tell by the murmurs moving through the crowd that this was out of the ordinary, but everyone got quiet when the door opened and he was escorted in. Everybody except Carmen.

"What the fuck?" she blurted.

"Will you please take the stand and state your name for the courts."

"My name is Raymond Vargas."

"Do you have an alias?" Judge Malloy asked.

"In the streets they call me Rocko."

"And why are you here today, Mr. Vargas?"

"To testify about the operations of Zayvion Miller as it pertains to what he's been charged with."

"Were you promised a deal for your testimony?"

"I was given full immunity from prosecution!"

"Well, Mr. Vargas, I regret to inform you that your deal has been rescinded." When the judge made that statement two cops came from the gallery to the stand and put Rocko in handcuffs, making sure to read him his rights before escorting him from the courtroom.

The judge had to bang her gavel several times to restore order, but when she did it was my turn.

"Mr. Miller, per the agreement you signed you must allocate the testimony you intend to give against Mr. Vargas." I stood up and took a deep breath, ready to play my role.

"Five years ago, a decorated police lieutenant that worked for the Fairfax County Police Department was brutally murdered on his way home from work. Mr. Vargas was the man who pulled the trigger, and I know this because he confided in me. He also told me the whereabouts of the gun."

"Ms. Watkins, were you able to verify any of this?" Judge Malloy asked.

"I was, Your Honor. Lieutenant Paul Blankenship was murdered as Mr. Miller described, and the weapon was recovered where Mr. Miller was led to believe it would be. Ballistics were run on the weapon and it's a verified match, and it also has Mr. Vargas fingerprints on it. We also found twenty thousand dollars in cash with Lieutenant Blankenship's prints on it, so this might be a robbery homicide."

"Based on DA Watkins verifications and the deal you signed, the charges against you are hereby dismissed, Mr. Miller. Am I to understand that his PO has already agreed to reinstatement?"

"He has, Your Honor," my lawyer replied.

"When that paperwork is complete you'll be released from the Department of Corrections custody. As for the court, you're free to go, but you must return to testify at the appropriate time," Judge Malloy ordered. And then the gavel banged.

To Be Continued...
Coming Soon

Stay Connected with Us!

Text **LOCKDOWN** to 22828 to stay up-to-date with new releases, sneak peaks, contests and more...

Thank you!

Aryanna

<u>Coming Soon from Lock Down Publications/Ca$h</u>
<u>Presents</u>

BOW DOWN TO MY GANGSTA

By **Ca$h & Jamaica**

TORN BETWEEN TWO

By **Coffee**

BLOOD OF A BOSS **IV**

By **Askari**

BRIDE OF A HUSTLA **III**

THE FETTI GIRLS

By **Destiny Skai**

WHEN A GOOD GIRL GOES BAD **II**

By **Adrienne**

LOVE & CHASIN' PAPER **II**

By **Qay Crockett**

THE HEART OF A GANGSTA **II**

By **Jerry Jackson**

TO DIE IN VAIN **II**

By **ASAD**

LOYAL TO THE GAME

By **TJ & Jelissa**

A DOPEBOY'S PRAYER **II**

By **Eddie "Wolf" Lee**

A HUSTLER'S DECEIT **II**

By **Aryanna**

<u>**Available Now**</u>

(CLICK TO PURCHASE)

<u>RESTRAINING ORDER **I & II**</u>

By **CA$H & Coffee**

<u>LOVE KNOWS NO BOUNDARIES **I II & III**</u>

By **Coffee**

<u>LAY IT DOWN **I & II**</u>

<u>LAST OF A DYING BREED</u>

By **Jamaica**

<u>PUSH IT TO THE LIMIT</u>

By **Bre' Hayes**

<u>BLOOD OF A BOSS **I II & III**</u>

By **Askari**

<u>THE STREETS BLEED MURDER **I, II & III**</u>

<u>THE HEART OF A GANGSTA</u>

By **Jerry Jackson**

<u>CUM FOR ME</u>

CUM FOR ME 2

CUM FOR ME 3

An **LDP Erotica Collaboration**

BRIDE OF A HUSTLA **I & II**

By **Destiny Skai**

WHEN A GOOD GIRL GOES BAD

By **Adrienne**

A GANGSTER'S REVENGE **I II III & IV**

THE BOSS MAN'S DAUGHTERS

A SAVAGE LOVE **I & II**

BAE BELONGS TO ME

By **Aryanna**

A DOPEBOY'S PRAYER

By **Eddie "Wolf" Lee**

WHAT ABOUT US **I & II**

NEVER LOVE AGAIN

THUG ADDICTION

By **Kim Kaye**

THE KING CARTEL **I, II & III**

By **Frank Gresham**

THESE NIGGAS AIN'T LOYAL **I, II & III**

By **Nikki Tee**

GANGSTA SHYT **I II &III**

By **CATO**

THE ULTIMATE BETRAYAL

By **Phoenix**

DON'T FU#K WITH MY HEART **I & II**

By **Linnea**

BOSS'N UP **I & II**

By **Royal Nicole**

I LOVE YOU TO DEATH

By Destiny J

I RIDE FOR MY HITTA

I STILL RIDE FOR MY HITTA

By **Misty Holt**

LOVE & CHASIN' PAPER

By **Qay Crockett**

TO DIE IN VAIN

By **ASAD**

<u>BOOKS BY LDP'S CEO, CA$H</u>

(CLICK TO PURCHASE)

<u>TRUST IN NO MAN</u>

<u>TRUST IN NO MAN 2</u>

<u>TRUST IN NO MAN 3</u>

<u>BONDED BY BLOOD</u>

<u>SHORTY GOT A THUG</u>

<u>THUGS CRY</u>

<u>THUGS CRY 2</u>

<u>TRUST NO BITCH</u>

<u>TRUST NO BITCH 2</u>

<u>TRUST NO BITCH 3</u>

<u>TIL MY CASKET DROPS</u>

<u>RESTRAINING ORDER</u>

<u>RESTRAINING ORDER 2</u>

<u>IN LOVE WITH A CONVICT</u>

<u>Coming Soon</u>

THUGS CRY 3

BONDED BY BLOOD 2

BOW DOWN TO MY GANGSTA